Urban Bigfoot

Deb Stratton

For When the Dream Finds you ...

First Printing: April, 2017

Printed in the United States of America

First Edition: April, 2017

ISBN-10: 1544134886

ISBN-13: 9781544134888

Introduction

For many years the search for Bigfoot has captured the attention of many worldwide. Bigfoot sightings have been reported in many Cities, States and Countries. The Bigfoot enthusiasm was launched many years ago. Each state or country has come up with their own nicknames to describe the hairy cryptid. What we call the beast is based on the sighting location. Will you spot any variation of the Hairy Being in your area? Oh, it is very possible. Encounters are reported across the United States and worldwide daily. The sightings have been in the wooded north and as far south as the swamplands.

If Bigfoot is everywhere why has one not been captured or clearly photographed? It could be because they are isolated and reserved.

"WE ARE HERE."

"YOU CALL US MANY NAMES AND HUNT FOR US TO SHOW OTHERS PROOF THAT WE EXIST.

BE CAREFUL WHAT YOU WISH FOR."

Chapter One

On such a beautiful morning, how can anyone expect but such a perfect day? As I woke up I began to make my rounds throughout the house, opening blinds, gathering laundry and such. I grabbed the bacon and my cast iron skillet, and I looked out to see the neighbors mowing and children playing in the streets. I love this time of day and I fill my mind with anxiety to see what the day will bring and how my life will unfold in all of its glory. If only at this moment I had realized my entire life would be different soon.

"Good morning" I said.

As the kids all started wandering into the kitchen to see what is cooking.

Sundays are the best days for family time in our home. The rest of the week was filled with work and my long hours working as an office assistant at the local nursing home. My afternoons were always spent at basketball games and doing homework. And it always made for a long day. Time to relax is definitely hard to come by.

My husband and I were divorced 4 years ago and in honor of keeping our family as dysfunctional as possible we still live together to raise our two children.

Marlie (age 11) and Devon (age 15). I had always felt lucky to have a home, a husband and such happy children. It is such a blessing. Stress sure takes it tolls on marriages and relationships in modern day and I was ready to give up as easily as he was but after rethinking it all we decided it was best to stay in the same house for the kids and for financial reasons.

I married Dave, right after my 20th birthday. He was the cool guy that played guitar. Which may be why our son Devon is talented in that area? I certainly am not. I stick with crafts and sewing. It is something easy to do in between working and family activities. Marlie plays basketball which is a time consuming sport. The Daily practices and games on weekends do not leave much time for my crafts. So I try to find something quick and easy to soothe my soul.

Having the clothes in the dryer was a chore marked off of my list for the day. I still had time to get my hair up and sneakers on. I sat down on my little wood bench and tied my laces.

I glanced over at the edge of the floor and seen some dog hair and realized that it had been a few days since I had swept. It will wait until I get back inside later.

I have wanted to spend more and more time outside when the weather was nice.

I recently turned 40 and I have put myself through my own midlife crisis. I tried to quit smoking on several occasions and found walking or exploring gets me out in the fresh air. I currently keep some hidden for rough days. I envy the mothers I see jog by in their cute leggings. They always have layered hair, while my hair looks like a rock star out of the eighties. It's all good. I may get there and I may not.

"Dave, I will be back in an hour, I am heading down to the dead end to walk the trail." I said in my hurried voice, so he does not think I am going to be gone too long.

Our modern home is in a subdivision with about 70 other homes. It is built on old farmland and it is surrounded by woods and ponds. I am happy to live in the back on the last road because it is a dead end. It actually helps keep the traffic down and it is nice and quiet. We opted for the ranch with one level so all of the bedrooms would be on one floor. It had worked well for us until one of the kids stay up with their music or TV's blaring through the walls.

I headed out the front door, checked my flower pots and tomato plants and hit the driveway in my new shoes and baggy sweatpants.

It is August and fall will be coming in soon. Missouri fall is unpredictable. It can last through November on a good year without a frost. Some years, the month of September is the latest I can grow any type of plant.

As I marched down the street, greeting others working in their yards, I regretted that I did not turn on my sprinkler. It is about 70 degrees this morning and with the heat increasing later in the day I would not be in a position to water until after 9pm. Oh well, no need to turn back. It will get done.

I often take my dog with me when I walk and today was one of those days I had left her behind. She is a wonderful dog. A large black lab named Solstice.

As beautiful as her name is, she can be quite a handful while waking. She is not really a family dog, she favors me and because of that I provide her with an unlimited amount of treats.

I was watching a show about dog training that implied that I am her pack leader. I had never become aware of this until watching her actions.

It is wonderful to me that this dog's only job in life is to love me. How great the world would be if that was the case with all human beings as well. Never knowing any other emotion but love would be peaceful.

I started picking up my pace with a slow run. My legs are long and I have always walked fast. I am not in the best of shape but get where I am going. I had seen the edge of the trees getting closer.

I found myself wishing I would have brought along my insect repellent, I have a great fear of tick bites. The pavement ended and I had made it to the start of the path. The sun was shining through the trees so flawlessly. The fresh scent and breeze was clean and so clear that I literally could not wait until I got home to open my windows that evening to enjoy it more. It is always so nice after the heat dies down later in the day.

"Good morning", I said to a passing jogger.

He was really rolling down the path with such experience. Almost everyone I see has headphones on so greeting them is usually just a wave.

I tend to be overly friendly, which to me is good, to some not so good. I just want people to know that I am happy and responsive. Some would say weird.

I love looking up in the trees. There were so many birds out. I pay attention as I have a great love for them.

My yard is filled with birdhouses and feeders. I am waiting to lure in a new family of finch that I can watch throughout the year.

We have Cardinals in our neighborhood but I have not had the luck of having them nest in my area. Life goal. Should I put a hashtag with that statement? I laugh and realize I think like I am online making a status update.

One remembrance I had which had always stuck with me was when I was about 10. It was the best memory. I recall I had gone with all of my friends to the woods to explore and make a clubhouse. The woods were always and still were very appealing to me. I often wonder why I have not found the chance to reside in the deep forests that surround most small towns here in my state. I long for a new life in a log cabin someday. One filled with beautiful fireplaces and pine furniture. It would be designed with open rooms and lots of warm rugs and windows. I have a plan in my wish book. I keep it hidden in my craft box for dreaming on rainy days.

Taking a look around I seen some mulched paths off of the rugged rock trail. I had not walked on most of the pathways. We have lived in this area for two years and I tried to stay on the rock paths for most walks.

I have no compass and I have seen too many horror films to venture off too far.

I am going to try a short footpath though because today I am feeling adventurous.

I am the great explorer of my forest and I am still feeling bad about leaving my dog behind. The shady path is still cool to me and I wish I had something to cover my arms.

I stumbled through the mulch path observing the crackle of broken twigs and wildlife around me.

It is absolutely amazing. I had watched a movie about trail walkers that were attacked by a bear. Why didn't I buy that bear repellent I had seen at the fish bait store? Are there bears in my area? Am I too old to out run one or climb a tree? I should have worn hiking boots. I am always hoping they come back in style for women. In high school we always had those light brown boots with the red laces. It was such a cool feeling to wear construction boots.

My new shoes are proving to be comfortable and I am happy that I had chosen these. I had almost put them back after the cashier told me that my coupon had expired.

I am standing now at the intersection of "wow you are completely lost" and "do not go this way". Hmmm which way do I go? My brain tells me to just turn around. I have only been out here 15 minutes and if I kept walking eventually I would stumble across a farm or something. My big adventure begins.

I look off to the west and it looks like rain may move in later. I really do not mind a little rain. The smell is soothing and calming to me. I have nothing else to really look forward to today but this great walk so bring it on. I feel the sun leave the tree tops and my shoulders as the clouds move in.

I decide to not go either way at the end of the path and jump across the little pebble creek.

Reminds me of the old streams where a speck of gold would glitter and catch your eye. Recreating the dream of being rich and finding the great fortune.

My collection of rocks has been growing from all of my walks. I usually bring home at least one. I often wonder why I love them so much. I spend a lot of time looking for the sparkly glimmering rocks. I also had an idea to do some rock painting for my garden and looked for some flat rocks that may serve my crafty purpose.

I should have brought along a bag with me. I found a few stones and set them to the side. I can always pick them up next time. If they are hidden well enough behind that old log I will come back by for my treasures.

The area seems untouched for quite some time. The trees are standing still without the breeze touching them. I noticed some areas around the trees where deer bed down and also some broken trees. The tree limbs looked like some sort of art display. They were large and heavy. Stacked and some were bowed out. There was also a line of trees that were growing horizontally. Some of the fallen trees were formed like an X.

Evidence of an old fire pit is still there with some old rusty cans. What a strange little area. Sometimes I had seen teenagers head out this way when we had first moved in and it may be a place where they used to hang out on weekend nights to party.

There was a heavy urine smell. I walked around a large oak and noticed two of the pines had been stripped of their bark. It was strange but interesting to me.

The pines were also pushed over into the forks of the other trees. I gave my best guess at this must be a previous attempt at building a secret fort or hideout by some kids.

I may bring my dog out next time to enjoy this walk. She loves the woods. It may be a good thing that she remained home if the clouds produce thunder she would be a bit frightened. She is the most anxious dog I had ever met. She was just a big bundle of nerves.

Jumping, splashing and leaping. There is nobody here to witness my childish playing. I am my own person. I feel like I am the only one on earth and this is my planet. Laughing and humming a bit I continue on. I am enjoying my new found freedom. My adventure is growing by the moment. I am half tempted to come back to this area and light a fire at night.

Too bad it is not mushroom season. I think this would be a great spot to pick up a Morel or two. Maybe I will mark it to find this area again someday. I have nothing with me but my clothes. Searching my person I notice that I have this crazy grouping of hemp bracelets on. I loved those hippie strings. I tied one to the branch.

Hemp lasts forever so it will blend in and also show me the way back to this area.

I tied one on a branch and try to use a sparkly rock to carve my name. E M short for Emily. Good enough for now. I always liked Em better anyway. I had always wished for my initials on a tree. Preferably it would be through the old fashioned method of my greatest love stenciling it on. This worked for me and I loved it. Carving into the bark less tree was much easier and did not require a large knife. Just a rock.

I was walking deeper into the path and I picked up my energy level enough to jump over some downed trees like an Olympic hurdler.

Hopping and skipping all the way until I fell.

I was falling through the ground rubbish, through some sticks. This is not my average being clumsy fall. It seems to me that I just fell about 20 feet into some sort of old well. My back is scratched and even though it has happened quickly, I feel like I hit my head.

After a quick glance I noticed my knuckles were bleeding a bit. It is not too far down and still judging by some episode I seen on the Hunting channel surely this is not really a big deal. I liked the survivor challenge and am angry at myself for not checking the ground strength while jumping around. Sometimes I amaze myself at my judgment calls in life.

Looking around it seems that it is a circle of rocks all around me. This hole that I have fallen into reminds me of an old well. It has to be.

I could climb 20 feet to get out if I could actually find something to grab a hold of.

At least there is no sign of water or rats. That would make my day go downhill really fast. I wish I had my phone. I felt that my photo opportunity for looking up out of this well at those trees would be an amazing profile photo. Bummer.

I started thinking of ways that would help me to get out of this hole. It seemed to me that nothing could really happen that was too terrible. I was sure there had to be other walkers and runners nearby. They were probably even close enough to hear my screams if I tried.

I am an anxious person that should have probably been medicated years ago and this may be the one time that makes me regret that decision. As I look up to devise some sort of plan, the light seems to be disappearing. Covered up more and all I see is more darkness. Screaming. "Help, please" I cry. "If someone is there, please come back".

I am sobbing and freaking out is my new middle name.

What is happening? What did I fall into? It is getting darker. Maybe it is just the clouds moving in. Why didn't I bring my dog or my phone?

I answer myself, "Because I am only a mile from my house". Panicking and breathing were in sync.

I am literally closer to my house than the local gas station. My thoughts are racing. Breathe. Breathe.

After I calm myself enough to stop crying and stay hopeful, I sit thinking that I have nothing to eat. Why am I always worried about food? What if I am here for a while? I have my water bottle hooked on, but how long will that last? And what about my fear of bugs and spiders? Is this a test? Did I fall into my worst fears test?

Was there a crazy person that followed me down the path? My thoughts are still running through my mind quickly and my heart is beating so fast I can barely function.

Was someone up there? NO, the answer is no. I know that no one was following me. I know that this is not a test. It is my bad luck and I have to find a way to get out.

I have no idea why the hole is covered up, thinking maybe it was a spring trap? For bears? Visions of a bear falling on my head any moment is real, and yes, I forgot to pick up that bear spray. I should have not watched that movie. Although at this point I am thinking what will get me out of this hole and save my life is the fact that I have watched those scenarios play out.

This is my day and fearfully my new challenge. Here I am sitting in a big hole that echoes and is now covered so no one can hear me. Next correct thing to do is pray. I should have done that first. "Please Lord, let me find a way out of this hole in the ground", I cry again. "Please, send someone to look for me". "Please?" I sit and wait. Nothing. Not that I expect an immediate answer to my plea for help. I think I have to accept the fact I may be here for at least an hour or so until someone misses me. While praying and crying, I am thinking maybe no one will miss me. I am having a conversation with myself that is not aiding me in any way.

About an hour has passed and I have discovered that this well or hole has excellent echo capabilities for singing. I never could really sing well, but enjoy singing loudly when no one is listening. I am really feeling quite paranoid at this point and even though I had never thought of myself as a claustrophobic person, I am definitely feeling the effects of being trapped and stuck in the hole. I am feeling cold and clammy even though it is a hot summer day.

I try to get a grip on anything I can to climb up, and there is just nothing useful. I hear something. I hear a voice. I am sure of it. It does not sound like it is above me though. It is sounding like it is at my level. Quiet I tell myself, like placing a glass to a wall to listen. I was listening more. What is that? I hear someone.

Maybe I am losing my mind. I knew that would happen eventually in my life.

But today? Really? I did not want to face that this morning. I had bacon and sunshine and now this.

I continue to feel around, and I discover something unusual. The bricks or stones that were used for this hole are old and rough. They have no moss or slimy residue. So maybe this is not an old well. Maybe it is a bear trap. I hear it again. It is a man. I hear him. It sounds distant but still not above me. Ear to wall, focus on the sound. What is that person saying? I cannot make it out.

I am interrupted again by the loud sounds of the wall opening. The wall next to my head opens and hands are reaching in.

Big hands. Very large animal like hands.

I am relieved to have some type of interaction with anyone, and am not thinking in my right mind. I am not leaving this hole by going up, but by going to the side.

I am crying and pulled through this opening only to discover a world no one could have ever dreamed existed.

Chapter Two

I am not sure how long I have been unconscious. I am not sure if I fainted from fear or if I hit my head. What is really happening here? It is warm, and the smell is almost farm like. I am surrounded by the same brick walls that were in that well. Not a modern day brick but a dirt packed brick wall. Glancing around I notice there appears to be others, many others, busy working. I notice tunnels and large work areas. There were some sort of small windows or holes. A small ray of sunshine was coming into my area. Gone again. The rain must be back again.

To the right I notice there seems to be other cot like beds, similar to the one I am laying on with others on them. Am I underground?

I find that the atmosphere is primitive. It is noisy, almost like being in one of the atrium buildings at our local zoo. Echo's and smells. Not really bad smells all at once but occasionally it will waft by.

There were conversations and laughing. I speak out, "hello"? A man on the cot just a few feet from me looks and is trying to give me some sort of eye contact. He does not speak back. "Hello, sir can you tell me what is happening?" I try again. "If you can hear me, please tell me something, anything? Why are we on these cots?" Should I get up? There is nothing holding me here. I could just get up and walk away.

I am not sure where the door is but there are hallways with mulch type flooring and vines. There are more holes and trickles of light coming down. I get a glimpse, of some type of movement. I want to scream and my eyes fill with tears. I really had wished I still smoked. I could really enjoy that right now.

I see a large man, which is more beastlike than anything. He was much taller than most men and very hairy. Well hairy is the simplest of words that I may use at this moment as I want to know what is going on and how to get back to where I was on my jogging path. I am fearful but not as panicked as I thought I would be. I am thinking more now of survival and how to get out.

The large manlike person is also not completely human in my eyes. He is close enough now to say something. He is holding something. I must be hallucinating because I am underground on a cot with a large hairy man standing near me with a smile. I must be crazy. I am going to talk to him. "Oh sir, may I ask you a few questions"?

The large man waves down the hall and a more feminine version approaches. His wife? Coworker? What is it? Something is deeply strange and as she comes into sight and gets closer I almost feel relieved. It was a woman. I can feel more comfortable with this situation. I am also still looking around continuously.

The others like me that are lying on their cots just stay there. They keep looking but do not speak. Why are they not speaking? They do not really look afraid or medicated. The young hairy woman approaches me. And she speaks! In a lovely voice that sounds like she has smoked for 50 years. She announces that her name is Barka.

I do not understand this. She has a name. She is living and breathing and speaking to me. I want her to tell me that this is all a mistake and that I will be dropped off at my house shortly.

But then Barka speaks again. "We are happy to have you here. You will be assigned a number tomorrow".

I am very happy that this hairy individual knows my language. This should make it much easier to communicate my feelings because I am going to panic soon. I am filled with anxiety that is turning into an excitement for the thrilling outcome of this story that I can run home with and tell everyone. That is if I can find a way to leave.

"Barka?" I said quietly. "May I please have some answers to my questions?"

I continue to ask about the area I am in. I ask about the others on the cots, the hallways, for water. I try to get as much as I can out, so she will choose to answer at least one. She continues to look at me and starts to speak.

Her eyes are so large and just look into mine with such concern and sadness. The smell is unique, not really disgusting, but woodsy. Almost like a pine tree. The words that come out are not what I could have predicted. She is very serious to say, that I have become part of her family now. She continues to explain that I will remain here and will be assigned a living space and a number. She turns again to walk away.

My mouth drops open. I have just heard with my own ears that I will stay here and will not be going home? I have a family. I have a home. A dog. I love my life. My eyes start to fill with tears again. It is coming, but I just keep looking at the others lying near me wondering what is going on. I am thankful that the female tree scented hairy being provided the information. Even though it was limited. It was really turning out to be such an emotional day.

I figured that I must try to stay calm and on the side of caution with this. This meant I must stand up with the others and follow Barka down the underground wooded path.

Walking down this hallway feels like actually being outside. And I am pretty sure we are down below the ground. There appears to be rooms etched into the hallway walls. Each with cots and wood, tree stemmed furniture. Very rustic and well designed. I feel damp. The air is chilling me. I feel sick.

I am walked to my cot and sat down by a touch to my shoulder. I looked across the hall path and seen a young man in jogging clothes placed on his cot as well. While I am looking at him, he looks into my eyes and I feel like he is trying to send me a message. Not all of the ones I have seen so far are taking this new environment well.

I hear screaming and crying. I also hear begging and urgent situations requiring other woods people to run down the mulch path.

I am not sure at this point how to describe Barka and the other man like creatures that are covered in an almost fake fur like body hair. It reminds me of something I would see on a costume. There are big differences in the humans that I know and them.

Their height for one thing, is at least a foot taller than mine. It looks varied and they must be very heavy. The muscular structure is perfect and amazing. There was more running. The woods people is my term at this point to try to describe what I am seeing when I look at these men and women in control. My hand is taken and a vine like shackle is placed on my wrist. I am not in a position to leave my four foot area.

There are oil lanterns hanging on the wall and what looks like to be some type of lighting running through the paths on the walls. I am confused. My head is unable to absorb what I am taking in.

There was a man across the path from me. He is tied to his area now as well. I watch him as he looks around and I am sure at this point that he may possibly be looking for a way to leave. I wish him good luck with that under my breath.

A large hairy person comes into my area and is carrying a wood box of metal pieces. I am sure at this point I am in a position to identify the male and female woods people. It would be some time before I would learn to identify them as some sort of Bigfoot or Sasquatch. I am still very much in shock at this point and I try to speak to what appears to be another female. She speaks!

She explains to me that she is here to provide me a number. She also says to me that there will be food provided soon.

I want to ask so many questions. I take a chance and ask if there is someone in charge, if there is someone I can speak to about leaving. She tells me that her name is Roota. That there will be a chance to speak with the others in a few days, and that it is best to remain silent until then. She advised me not become difficult and that we are all there for a reason. What reason?

So let me rehash this so I can try to comprehend it. I was very close to my home in a wooded area. I fell in what I know now was a trap. This was a trap that was intentionally set to collect me and bring me down to the woods people. I was sure that my running path would not lead many to where I was and that meant to me that possibly there were multiple traps in many areas.

I did not recognize the others that were on the cots earlier, and I feel that I would have if they were from my area. I am not sure that I woke up in the same area that I was near when I fell in trap. I may have been taken down other paths.

Snap. I hear her preparing my number. The metal tag shows the number 441 on it. It looks like a smaller version of the plastic tags they put on farm animals. She carefully and gently grabs my earlobe and snaps in the side cartilage. It felt like when I was young and had gone to get my ears pierced for the first time. It stings a little and I am also really worried about germs.

It was a dumb thing to worry about at this point but I would hate to get an infection while I am rope vined to a cot in a dirt cubicle on a bark filled path underground. I may be dreaming. Maybe this is not even happening.

It is real, I am here. I am thinking that keeping my mental stability may be important and that I need to pay attention and stop looking for reasons that this could not be happening. Snap. She is preparing to place a second tag on my left ear now. She turns my head gently and takes my earlobe to place the second tag on. I thank her for her gentle touch and she looks at me for a moment.

She is now glaring into my eyes. She is rubbing my forearm with tenderness. I almost feel like she cares about me. She tells me that I am welcome here and that she wishes me a good and safe visit.

Her English is perfect! I am so bewildered by the small details of what is around me. Ape like humans that speak like they are college educated.

I would have had an easier time accepting an alien spaceship in the yard that would have taken me to another planet, than I can believe this.

I wait until my path neighbor gets his number and then when the coast is clear I ask his name. I tell him my name and he responds with an angry voice. His name is Collin. He goes on to tell me that he is from a town that is about 40 miles from mine. He is 23 and very athletic looking. I did not really want to create a situation that would be a reason for reprimand so I kept it simple. I told him I was hungry.

He told me that he also believed his mother Staci was here somewhere as well. That made me sad.

I am not able to locate my water bottle and was sure I had it when I was pulled from the well. It was clipped on my side. The water bottle was a gift from my daughter and it never seemed so important until right this moment.

This brought a huge flood of emotions flowing through me, realizing that I may not see my family for a few days or months.

Chapter Three

Above ground the police are at my home. While I am vine tied and sitting in a dirt room, the law enforcement officer is taking a report from Dave. He will be questioned while the police check the area and mark the trails that I traveled down. There will be many neighbors throwing accusations that he had hurt me. There are also new rumors that I was abducted by someone that was taking women statewide.

I am trapped. My disappearance had brought a large police and FBI presence to my home and neighborhood. The story will be on the news for days. The police mark the woods. Find my bracelet. Follow my trail until it goes cold. Flyers are printed and placed on poles and grocery store doors. I am missing. My family is experiencing a very new life up there and I am unable to tell them that I am alive and missing them.

I look over at my new friend across the path. We are silently waiting for food and water. There is not a lot of noise to judge the other's activity by. I am struggling with the desire to know what time it is. I am sure I have been here 2 days. Maybe 3.

I am not sure how long I was asleep or unconscious. I notice near my cot there is an unusual wood crate. I am able to get to it easily and stand up to touch it. It feels so great to stand and walk around. I remove the lid and discover that it may be the modern built outhouse that I have been seeking. There is nothing like having a toilet 3 feet from where I sleep.

I am feeling more like a prisoner and still am having major confusion about where I am and what or who is keeping me here. I want to yell for Barka. She was kind. I am afraid that if I yell I would be deemed unruly and that there could be consequences. I did not want to stand out.

Just as I sit on the crate to relieve myself I hear voices. I am discovered by a new female hairy person and am given a stitched up braided sack of dried meat. I am guessing that the ones responsible for my visit here are not vegetarians. I am happy to have some protein and am also given my water bottle back with cool water in it. I also see my neighbor Collin getting a meal as well. I wait for her to get out of view before I attempt to stand up from the box I am using as a toilet.

Moving back to the cot I sit quietly and eat slowly. I have no idea again how long it had been since I had eaten and do not want to become sick. I am not a fan of jerky or dried meat so trying to stomach this was not easy for me. I decided to keep some and I rolled it up in my sleeve just in case I would need it at a later time.

Somewhere along the line I have been stripped of my shoes and socks. I gently tuck my legs together and try to pull my stretchy sweat pants over my feet to get some warmth. It is not cold, just uncomfortable for me. I am definitely one of those comfy blanket kinds of girls. I am not just one with my cot which was some sort of canvas and no other extras. NO pillow or blanket. It was just me. I feel the need to rethink what I have seen so far. I took a good look at Barka. She was not human but very close. Her facial expressions and use of her hands were the same as mine. Her size was much more magnificent than any human I have ever seen. She seemed smaller than some of the others I had seen go by. Maybe this was a female trait.

NO clothing that I could see and there was so much body hair that I could not see any specific body parts. It appeared that she was covered in some areas with a covering that matched her hair. It was maybe out of modesty or necessity. It was easy to see why they would all be comfortable with the cool air.

Flashbacks of old movies and shows from my childhood kept coming to mind. I was not sure if those memories would help me uncover the mystery of this mess I was in. I am scared and intrigued at the same time. I was frightened to fall asleep because I am not sure what will happen to me if I do. There surely must be some purpose to collecting people and bringing them down to the world below the woods that I am in.

Maybe I am not even under the woods any longer. I could be anywhere by now. They could have taken me somewhere while I was knocked out.

Barka comes in. Oh such relief to see her. It almost feels to me like when you start a new job and the other new person is the only one you know so you feel comfortable with them right away. I feel like I know her. She sits on the ground in front of me and begins to tell me that after everyone in this ward is finished eating we will all be taken to a group room.

I ask her where I am. She tells me a story to tell me that her family is very large and has been populating the earth for hundreds of years. That the culture is unique to nature and the underground is the safest place to dwell. I thank her for giving me that information even though I have no idea what she really means. I am repeating myself in my thoughts, underground, surrounded by large hair covered half human and half forest beast?

I am thankful for the chance to get more answers and as she walks over to the area near me, I study her gait. I see that she walks well. She has animal like feet and hands only to the point that they are thick skinned and larger than mine. It is almost primitive in looks, but very modern in intellect. She is actually very well versed and I feel like I must high on something to even believe what I am seeing.

I look at the walls while I wait. They are dirt but molded. They are not crumbly. They are packed in and formed. Someone spent a lot of time digging these out I am sure.

I see no modern conveniences other than the evidence of my cot and the lanterns. Also the design of some areas I had seen before I got to this area seemed more advanced. The brick walls were not in this section. I see nothing electronic.

NO cell phones or televisions. NO noises of any sorts that would indicate beeping or computer like.

I am greeted by a group of humans and hairy people and waved to come along, as my vine is removed by Barka. There are 5 others like me in clothing and 6 hair covered. Of the 5, I am the only female. I guess finding women in the woods alone is more rare than men. I must be a real gem.

We all walk together silently to the end of this mulched walkway. It sounds like a fan or wind tunnel is

Ahead. Some sort of air flow. The blowing is definitely making the odd stench more apparent and it reminds me of a trip to petting zoo. Stale. Unclean. I arrive at the group room which must be for frequent gatherings. There were amazing pieces of natural tree and stick furniture everywhere. I would almost say this could possibly be a great hit at any rustic craft store. There is a large table made from a tree. In front of this room there are rows of chopped tree trunks, in the form of stumps. It is very similar to the old campfire ones.

We are all sitting while a conversation at the table became intense. In a strong and sensitive man voice, the bearded one says to us that his name is Stem. He would be speaking to us as a group and then one on one. I feel like I am at work meeting ready to ask questions. I have so much I want to say. Is this the right time?

The commotion begins. Noises begin out in the hallway path and start entering the room as many others start to fill the area. I only see the 4 other similar beings to myself. All others are still displaying the hairy overgrowth that I cannot stop looking at. I am starting to put things together slowly and it is very hard for me to even believe that this is real.

There was Ground Pounding, stomping and running by some coming into the room. The metal lights that are hanging begin swaying and small dirt chunks from the walls begin to fall. To describe it best would be primitive but very well designed. I am taking it all in, and trying not to get anxious or nervous. I just want to leave and run out of here. I am guessing that the only way I will ever find my way out of here it to blend in and become a cooperative person. I will do what they ask and hope that the reward will lead me out of this place eventually.

The room fills with odd chanting that is almost animal like. I relate the human hairy figures in the room to this type of breed.

I am sure that they must have some history of caveman relatives. I am thinking it through, woods people, hairy individuals. I believe that this must be some sort of relation to a Bigfoot or Sasquatch. In Missouri the legend was always called MoMo. The grandparents of my generation had always told the stories of running from the woods after seeing such a creature. I had heard of sightings in the area multiple times and always chalk it up to the types of people that look for a story to make the news. After all, most of the sightings never panned out to really becoming anything other than a tale.

There is a photo, a sighting, a story, and then nothing because there is never any proof. It is almost like the Bigfoot disappears instantly.

This makes sense to me now, as to how this could happen. If what I am seeing is proof that they exist. The underground homes they have made for themselves has provided a quick escape from any hunter or individual looking for a news story.

The room is now full. The smell is real. The warmth from the body heat all around me is real. There is really no attention being paid to myself or the others that were unvined and brought to this area. We just sit on these stumps waiting. A strong tall figure stands at the front of the room and begins speaking. Stem. He would like to welcome everyone to the gathering and is offering all a chance to get a good look at us. Pointing and speaking, it feels almost like an auction.

Whispering and staring. I am feeling like I am about to be carried off to another unknown place. The room has become louder and a female takes a hold of the hand of another human man that is on a seat by me. He is walked off leaving just me and another man. Another group comes forward and takes the remaining male to the back of the room and they exit down the path. I am left alone with this group. There seems to be a disruption. They are arguing. Many are pointing and I am being touched and my hair was being sniffed to assure one that I was OK.

The fighting continues until the head of the meeting yells loudly announcing that everyone should leave. This is a problem as there are many that are disputing his decision. Some large hairy ones escort others out of the room.

I am left on the stump with only Stem standing in front of me. He looks at me continuously into my eyes. He sits on the ground in front of me and says to me that I will be safe and I will be going with him.

I feel my eyes swell up with tears. I try to be as calm as possible and he can see that I am upset. I look back at him. Looking around at the dirt walls and tree stumps. I do not feel warm. I am once again feeling damp and cold here. I miss the comforts from my life like quilts and pillows. I miss clean clothes. I need sunshine on my face.

He tells me that this will be my new home and that he does hope that I will find some comfort. He then goes on to tell me that he saved me from some of the other owners that wanted to take me to make me work for them. I believed him and was about to find out that he was waiting himself for a female for a very long time. I was that female.

He said he saw something in my eyes and could not

allow the others to take me away. He took my hand and we walked towards the entryway into the mulched path. We are not walking in the direction that I have originally come from before this gathering. The path was taking us more downhill than we had previously been on.

We walked together for more than thirty minutes. The scenery changed and we entered a large general area filled with an underground pond and vines. There is a waterfall and small, very small hairy people playing. Are these children? There are cook stoves made of stone and a small fire.

There are females laying out strips of meat on wood tables. I am assuming this is what I was fed when I was taken to my original little cave. It was some sort of dried meat or jerky. That is what it reminded me of. There is also a large amount of meat on another table. I am sure they consume large amounts based on their sizes and I see no other types of food.

There is the feel of family here and happiness. Everyone around me in this area is well versed and friendly. They are all working hard together to complete their daily chores. I just stare in confusion. I want to accept that this is real, but cannot.

I feel like I will wake up any moment and would be at home again. Stem is still grasping my hand gently and is not aggressive at all.

He has not put the vine back on my wrist and is allowing me to walk at my pace even though his stride is massive and he could easily make one step up to my 5.

He is pleasant and gentle. Soft. He takes my arm and moves me to the front of him as we step into a doorway of beauty. This large area is filled with such an array of nature filled trinkets and other random items. I feel myself turning to look in every direction just to take it all in. It is pleasant and clean. I see his resting area and living quarters. A small fire pit area. There are many different types of wood and stick furnishings surrounding the perimeter of the room which is huge.

Stem tells me softly not to be worried or frightened. He continues on by telling me that I will reside here with him as his worker and he will in turn for my services take care of my wellbeing. I do not really want to do this but I am strangely fascinated with him. He is actually very nice and seems to be good company so far.

I am still confused as to what day it is. I have been in

captivity for several days at the least. I can tell by the way my hair feels oily and my teeth feel unbrushed.

Stem motions to follow him and we walk out and down the path to the common area. I am sitting in a corner area taking in the surroundings when a female comes up.

She places a container of water on the table for me and pats my hand like an old grandmother would do. She looks middle age and content with what she is doing here. Stem takes what he would like from the tables and motions for me to take my new items and follow him. We walk back to the sleeping area without any talking.

I am attempting to come up with some sort of name to actually call my new captors. I realize more and more that they must be a creature of the woods and the best that I can do is call them a Bigfoot. Do they know they are a mythical creature of the forest that people have talked about for many years? I have never really been one to believe in such things, including conspiracy theories or ghosts.

I had always wanted to believe and thought I may eventually stumble across some sort of proof that would intrigue me enough to search for more information. I would not have guessed that the type of proof my brain required to believe in such a thing would come along while taking a jog in the park. It did start making sense to me a little more.

Last year there were other men and women missing in our area. There were also many missing over the past years in all areas of the United States. There was really never an explanation. Most people just figured it was due to abductions or the increase in human trafficking. I always had thought it was uncaptured scripted killers that just hid in our society. I must have been wrong. This may be the final clue in solving hundreds or thousands of missing person cases.

Some missing people were found and others were not. Is this what had become of them? I had to find out more.

I fell into a trap and if there were more traps in multiple areas, this underground haven I have landed myself in could possibly be very large. It could be miles and miles wide. There could be hundreds, if not thousands of Bigfoot here as well.

I have discovered that there is an unlimited amount of food and water for everyone here. There are sleeping areas and intelligent beings living in a world that they have designed. The vision that I see for them is a very well organized army of the hairy ones that have rules and order. A very similar life to what humans have. Well almost. We have sunlight and fresh air. We also have money and hair removal products. I am shocked that I even just thought that due to the dark place that my thoughts are in right now. I have decided once again to cooperate and find a way home. I have no other solutions at this time.

As I sit here I looked at my hands. I started cleaning out the dirt from my under my fingernails and I still had a chill. It is not really uncomfortable it is just not the type of warmth I am familiar with. I glance down at my feet and am sorry that I had ever complained about wearing old worn out socks or shoes. At this point, I would happily take whatever was given to me.

Stem enters a small room and several minutes later he comes back out. He is very smooth and kind. He comes to the corner quickly to take a seat on a large bench. He asks my name. He asks if I am in need of food.

I look at him and quietly say my name and that I would be happy to have some more food. I am still holding the items I was given and start drinking while he sits down. I also point to my feet and tell him that I would like a covering or a blanket.

I needed something to warm my body. He sends out a whistle that some would say was close to being ear shattering and minutes later a hairy Bigfoot woman brings in a burlap bag and leaves it at my feet.

Chapter Four

Inside my sack is more dried meat. I have not determined what type it is. It must be beef or venison. It is dark and is so perfectly dried that it appears to have sparkle like crystals on it. I was hoping for some fabric to cover my feet and at this moment I have realized that everything is about food. I rip off a piece to eat quickly and grab the extra jug of water out of the sack to feel more refreshed. I notice there is a small fire burning across the room with some type of grate over it. A rusty tin can is sitting on top of it. To the right is a sleeping area and a few small dug out rooms with other items in them. I ask Stem if he could give me more information on who he is and where I am at. I really would like to know what type of plan to make. I am not sure why I am here. He only says I will know all of the answers I seek in due time.

Closing my eyes, I try to listen to the noises down the pathways. There are no doors and I can hear a lot of talking and yelling. I cannot hear what the others out there are saying clearly enough to make out words. "Stem, I am not explaining myself very well. I need to know why I am here and who you are." I sip on my water while I wait for an answer. He is busy making some sort of vine knot. Hopefully not the same type that had me restrained in the previous area I was in.

He looks at me and says, "You are in our world now. We are the ones that are spoken of for many years by your people." He continues to tell me that for the many years of his life that he and his large family had existed without harm. I understand when he tells me that he has never been caught or harmed by anyone.

I had heard of a story many years ago when I was camping, a story of a large hairy man that broke limbs and ran through the woods. It sounded terrifying then and now it is really blowing my mind. I raise my eyebrows at him and say that I would like to help in any way that I can. I also asked that he assure me that I could leave and go home.

At that moment Barka came into the room with another female and ask if they may take over the conversation. Stem complies and thanks them for visiting. "Emily, Stem has taken you in, to keep you safe. You have fallen into our world and for many decades human men and women have searched for us." She continues to tell me, that they are a large group that expands in the earth, what we call the underground. They live in sections and it branches out for many miles under many areas. I have spent limited time above searching for food, supplies and sometimes just out of curiosity.

It was not until about 20 years ago, that they had the gift of learning our language. A visitor from another area was brought down to study and had offered to teach them how we communicate with each other through words. I notice that there is no slang. The English being used is primitive and straight to the point. Yet impressive.

"We have no other way to discover and learn without you." She continues to explain. "In our family we have thousands spread out. We raise children and work hard just as you do above the ground."

I was actually very interested in the information that she was giving. I felt like I had discovered something wonderful and would be famous the world over for what I could take back and tell. According to Barka the humans that have been captured all have jobs that they do here. Many are used to dig out additional tunnels and smooth walls. I notice the fine detail that is carved into every area that I can see. The human touch is obvious. Instructions must have been given over the years to them for furniture building, drying meats, learning English and grooming.

There is an odor, but it is mostly the odor of stale indoors air with a touch a dampness and if I may say, similar to my wet dog. Stem and the others I have met all seem to have brushed hair and it is so clean it is almost shiny. Not matted down or similar to a dread lock. It actually looks groomed.

I have noticed that they all have teeth that are very real and similar to mine. Her eyes are very large compared to mine and her nose is much wider. I don't want to tell her that I want to leave. While she is speaking I remain silent. While I am staring at her that is all I can think about though. I am thinking about going home.

Barka then introduces me to the new female she has arrived with earlier. Her name is Pine and she is a medicine worker. This is a Bigfoot doctor? Pine explains to me that some residents here are very advanced and some still stuck back in the old days. They refuse to grow or educate themselves. She also says that their family is very similar in many ways.

They have discovered that the most successful family members are those that have bore a child with the humans. She continues on to provide examples of what some of their great hunters have accomplished that have actually bred with Native American Women. Her words are keeping me in a speechless daze. I feel the tears again. The type of tears that just fill up your eyes enough to make things foggy. I knew if I blinked they would run down my cheeks, so I tried to look away.

I wanted to clarify what she was saying. "Are you telling me that I was brought here to become a worker?" I wait.

She replies simply, "NO you have not. Originally yes, and then Stem saved you." I will be saved for another purpose at a later time. As she stands up and steps back for a moment, they speak in a quiet voice. It was almost a kind and friendly kind of chat that you see old friends conduct on the streets in passing.

As they finish up their conversation, Barka is kind in letting me know that if I need anything to leave a message with Stem and they will tend to my needs as quickly as possible. Well, I need to be free. That would be my only need at this moment.

I am going to just get that thought out of my head for a day or two to avoid upsetting myself. I am shocked, surprised, bewildered, overwhelmed and amazed at what has unfolded here today. I am in Bigfoot territory and nothing at this moment is going to change that. I feel so upset that I cannot change what is happening. I have no control of anything that is going on around me and I have no clear instructions on what I am supposed to be doing or what I can and cannot do. I set my sack to the side and stand up. I decide that I am going to glance out into the pathway to see what is going on out there.

I get closer to the doorway and see to the left the pathway to the large area with the waterfall. There are many others down there talking and small hairy children playing and running. I cannot hear the words but the sounds echo down the pathway well.

The weight that they carry around is causing a rumbling and trail of noise. They are solid and strong. Their intelligence is more than anyone above the ground would have ever guessed. I am anxious to go and explore. I will wait though. I will wait until it is a good time, or until Stem or Barka tell me what I am to do next.

A day went by, then another. I was given a cot to rest on and the sacks kept coming with my daily meat meal and water. The pathways were filled with busy beings traveling to and from their home areas, I am guessing. I curled up on my cot just watching them live their day to day lives.

I lifted my arms high to stretch for a few moments. Sitting and laying so much was starting to take a toll on my health. I longed for a walk through my neighborhood or a jog through the park. I am sure of one thing and that is that after seeing what I have seen and knowing about this Bigfoot Culture down below I may never be able to live life above again without the fear of being taken or trapped. I would love to get a message to all of those Sasquatch Hunters that are laughed at because no one believes.

The earth shook as I sat and nibbled on my meal. The heaviness of their steps in the pathways made the lighting sway and the walls rumble. I used my sacks to pull together a covering. It was a handmade blanket of sorts. Even though it is not filled with cotton batting and fabric that was store bought it was bringing me a sense of comfort.

Stem entered the room smiling. It was a big creepy friendly smile. I was curious as to what could be causing him so much happiness. He had spent much of his time going in and out of the room doing what must be his work.

So, I asked. "May I ask why you are enjoying this day so much? And also may I ask if you track days down here? I am wondering how long I have been here and if this is where I will be staying."

I stood up and stretched again and then sat down on my cot with my hand made blanket and waited for his response.

"I am your new keeper." Stem announced gently.

"My family comes from many years of Tree Warriors and we have chosen to bring you into our family. You are a gift from above."

I laugh just a bit and reply, "I am flattered that you have chosen me, and a bit humbled. However, you must know that I am in unfamiliar territory and lived a very different life than the ways I have seen your family living here."

I wait for him to respond. I am impressed with the language and intelligence he presents me. He walks over to the small fire and puts some dark colored rocks on it. The rocks are dark black and they look just like the coal I have seen in stores during the holiday season.

As he moved them around with a large stick, he turns and smiles again.

He says, "Your name is Emily and part of your name is also part of my name." According to the tree fathers you are my chosen one. I will take care of you and your needs. You will be shared with no one. I will not allow the others to breed you or use you as a worker."

I am very nervous and my hands are grasping each other. They feel sweaty. I want to cry and beg to leave. I am afraid that if I do this it would make him angry. So I told him nothing.

An older hairy man came in the room and said hello. Stem asked him to leave us for just a few more minutes. He stepped back out into the pathway. He moved closer to me and reached out for my hands. I complied and gently he pulled me to my feet. His scent, his touch and his eyes were captivating.

His voice gently says, "Em let's go meet the others. I would like to see your face filled with a smile and not fear."

I walked with him hand in hand to the pathways and even though he towered over me by at least 12 inches. I felt safe and excited to see what was out there. We walked and walked until I thought we would have never seen anyone ever again. Suddenly we came upon a new area to me filled with many others.

As we turned the corners of the path, a young one ran up and begged Stem to run with him. It seemed to be a game they were playing in the large area where everyone gathered.

I looked in all directions and I have seen hairy men and women talking, cooking, and turning to look in my direction. I had also seen 2 other Bigfoot males with human females. They were beautiful and even though they were not from my subdivision, I am sure they were from my area. I smiled as they smiled at me. They did not look harmed or scared. They actually seemed happy and adjusted.

One female was braiding her gentleman's fur. She seemed to be grooming him and he laughed and spoke to the others around him while she tugged on his hair and warned him not to move. Amusing... Were they a couple?

The facial features of those men are very human like, and although the hands and feet are quite massive, the similarities are there. I am starting to wonder if Stem and these other men are part human. The hair or fur covers their bodies perfectly and I can see that there are some grooming techniques they are using to cover their private areas. Something that I was not wanting to notice or see, but it was there.

I stood back when he announced my name. Everyone smiled and said hello. There was one female that was not human that was glaring at me. She did not want to acknowledge my presence. This was ignored by the others and the pride in Stems voice kept the group happy.

I was his gift and he was beaming with joy despite the warrior inside of him that could be the complete opposite. Stem walked to a table and retrieved a braided hair band. It was made from flowers and he placed it gently on my head. I noticed the other females also had them on. It was Very lovely. I felt lovely. I also felt a bit strange. Stem says his farewells to the group of others and we headed down the path once again. We are not walking in the same direction that we came from so I am excited to see more.

He says to me, "I will not leave you alone or at risk of feeling helpless. I will share with you my family and my home. What I am and what I have will live inside of you." I smile and thank him.

He takes my hand once again and begins to explain what he is showing me. "The pathways travel for many miles in all directions, each pathway leads to other areas where groups of Tree Warriors or in your words, Bigfoot families live. We have leaders just as you do. We have elders and children. We have jobs that are assigned to each member of the groups and we have no currency. Here we live without greed or hate. We only know how to survive and to care for who we love."

I am without words, so he continues. "Our culture is real and unchanged in many ways, and yes we have been seen by humans. We travel alone as to leave out the risk of exposing our families and groups to the large population above."

I just had a deep understanding for what he was describing to me. A large underground life filled with primitive hair covered beings. That also included evolving and breeding with humans. In that moment, I became saddened. I was sad that I was forced to leave my happy life above to come down below to satisfy their growing culture. I kept my sadness in and he discovered it quickly.

Right then he lets go of my hand and takes me into his large arms. He rubbed the back of my hair and then straightened out my flower crown and began walking again. I was walking where he walked and stopping where he stopped. He continued to show me other rooms, homes and areas. There were kitchens and many rooms in every direction. We then came upon a very well-lit area.

It was a medical room. I am sure this is where he was intending to take me from the beginning. Barka was there with her assistant.

She says to Stem, "You may leave her with me while you do your work, I will see to it that she is returned by nightfall."

Stem releases my hand and smiles. He thanks Barka and leaves the area to the pathway on the right. I felt alone again and only Barka could provide me the answers that I needed to make it through this traumatic change in my life.

"Please have a seat Emily I am to provide your exam and your introduction to our elders." She said. Then she continued, "I will start at the beginning with the questions that are most commonly asked of me and then if you would like to talk more, I will be happy to answer your questions."

Barka continued to check my hair and skin. She looked closely at my nail beds and knees. She looked at my teeth. Checking and rechecking my body and placing a finger on my ear tag. The ear tags never became infected. I am shocked of that. I am instructed to take a flat moss like tablet that looks like compressed dirt.

Knowing that I am underground and dirt is great in abundance does not surprise me that I am actually going to eat it. I am told it is nutritional and will help keep me healthy. I am also briefed on how to maintain my cleanliness and female issues. I am concerned about this. I am concerned about my mental wellbeing and my anxiety.

As she paced around the room gathering items to place in yet another sack, she continues to tell me that there are many others I will meet from up above. That most are workers that have chosen to stay and become a part of their communities and of course some are also what she had previously described to me as breeders. There is no way to leave without disclosing what they have protected for so many years. That needs to be eliminated from my thoughts. She nudges me and asks me kindly to stand up. There is a wall with marks on it and I am backed up to it so that she can see how tall I am. 5 foot 8 inches is what I am thinking and have no idea what kind of measuring system could be used down here. The measuring marks looks like a collection of all of the humans that have passed through this room over the years.

I am guessing there are more than a hundred marks and they all have a number next to them. My number is then added next to mine. I am officially part of the collection.

"Barka, can you please tell me more? Can you tell me how old you are? If you are a Bigfoot or Sasquatch species, how long have you lived here? Do you know that people up above do not know about your homes down underground?"

There that should get me a few answers. She says that up until just a few years ago, there was no developed system for marking what we call days or years. When that was introduced by a human that was brought down, the learning began. The teaching was at first very difficult learning how to identify objects with vocal words. At that time she was just old enough to find a mate, and so she is estimating that she is about 30 years old.

Well. She stood in thought for a moment and then said, "I have only been up above one time, and that was when I had begged my elder to take me.

The travel is very limited up there and it is only for hunting and collecting items that we are in need of." She continues, "When I had gone up, we ran through trees and gathered items. I wanted to spend the time I had looking at everything. I wanted to see the sun and animals. I wanted to see buildings and people."

In her sadness she continued once more to say, "Your world is filled with noise and fear. It is very busy and according to our history, the world up above has

never been able to accept our species as intelligent or equal. We are hunted and leave behind a legacy of something that is frightening and harmful."

I am obsessed with her words. I want to hear more. I want to comprehend what she is saying and convince myself that all is well. Suddenly I grabbed her in fear as a loud painful scream echoed down the pathway. It was a scream that sounded like pain and torture had just become someone's fate. I continued to listen in hopes that it would stop and then the pounding and thumping through the walls and pathway began. Shaking all around until I seen several large warriors run by. There must be an emergency. Something is happening and I am frightened.

Barka gently removes my hand from her hair covered forearm and looks out of the doorway.

She glances each way and says to me, "Let's get finished up so we can get you back to your warm cot." She then takes out a large wood box and fits me with some shoes. I am happy to see mine there and point out the ones I had come with.

There are also pants and sweatshirts in the second box and I fill my sack with all that she allows me to have. I am thrilled about the snow hat that I see. I feel like I have just won the lottery. She then tells me, that she wishes me well. We may see each other from time to time and when I choose to mate or bare an infant she will care for me.

Chapter Five

I wake up with Stem and Barka standing over me. I am on my cot and my sack of treasures is next to me. I am told by Barka that I had become faint and that Stem had carried me back to my cot in his area. I know that the words mate or child rearing may have made me collapse from stress or fear. I had no words to describe the feeling that came over me and felt disgusted by the thought of it all.

I thanked Barka and Stem and ask to rest for a few minutes on my own. They comply and walked over to the entryway to talk more. I just want to lay here. I just want to drift away and give up. I want to cry. I want to go home. I fall asleep. If only for a moment.

Just as quickly as I had fallen asleep I wake up. I was looking around for my sack blanket and my new bag of goodies. I really want to wear that snow hat and sweatshirt. I dig through the bag and quickly put on my new items, feeling like I just left a shopping mall. I sit up and look over across the room.

Stem is sitting there alone tinkering with a homemade wood flute made out of several hollowed out tree stems. He is using a dried brown vine to wrap around it. I sit weeping with the thoughts of being here for the rest of my days. Stem senses my sadness and asks me to come and sit with him.

He tells me that I am free to explore the area and even take the pathway to the common area for bathing and grooming but to please take him along at all times. I feel his sincerity and thank him once again for his kindness. I am at a loss at what to actually say or do because in my world, up there, there is constant entertainment. There is always something to do. There is no TV here. There is nothing to do here. At least when I go camping there is something to enjoy. Like fishing or building a bonfire. Cooking or cleaning that would be time consuming.

I ask Stem if the entire community eats this dried meat. I ask what it is. I spend all of my waking hours wondering about everything. I could explore like he has offered. I may feel better if I was getting some of my energy out.

I really miss sleeping with the sound of a fan and white noise. Something to just take the echo away and silence that makes my ears ring.

He continues to work on his project with extreme contentment. I sit and watch for a few minutes and ask what he is creating. He looks at me with half a smile and then blows into the end with such force that I am sure the entire thing will fly across the room, but it doesn't. It makes a noise, a tune. A strange little tune that makes no sense to me and I am sure at this very moment what to do. While he blows into the ends, I start humming.

I hum a little and he looks out of the corner of his eye while I begin to sing. I sang the first song that came to mind and it was goofy and silly but fun. "Don't worry, bout a thing...cause every little thing is gonna be alright." I continued singing and Stem could not get enough of my off note singing. I just kept going until I ran out of words, and even though I had always loved that song, I had just realized I did not know half of the lyrics.

We sat for a good hour or two just blowing on that homemade musical pipe and I kept singing making up words. I was really enjoying it so much that I did not want it to end. But as they say, all good things must come to an end. He lets me know that it is time to eat. I have noticed that there are no real meal times which surprise me due to the size of the warriors that live here. I have strayed from using Bigfoot or Sasquatch due to their own terms that were introduced to me. I know that they do not have even a clue as to how many names humans have come up with to describe the sightings in the woods over the years. I wonder what they call us. I may put that on my list of curious questions to ask.

I graciously extend my hand as he stands up to escort me to the common area. I am not as nervous about it as I was the first time. I am hoping the same "people" are there so I can feel at ease and not awkward. We walk together and as we walk I sing a little quietly to make him chuckle. We enter the area grinning at each other, which is fun until I see that female hairy woman staring at me again.

Oh, another question to put on my list. Do I dare ask who she is? Maybe she is just an unhappy mean being. I do not know her name so I quickly decide to call her Hairy Mary. Finding humor in all things is a small gift of mine, it keeps pulling me out of the bad place my thoughts lead me to.

We take a seat by the waterfall that flows into a pond. The pond must be some type of an underground cave. Because of the way it pools there with rock behind it. The area reminds me of a trip to the caverns. It may also explain the difference in temperatures in this area. It feels warmer, maybe from the steaming water. As we sit we are greeted by many and along comes a female human with a couple of sacks. What else should I have expected? In the sacks are dried meat and some type of fungus, not the morel type but similar. I am leaning towards a firm no on eating this, and tuck it back into my bag. Problem solved no unwashed earthy mushrooms for this girl.

The server says her name is Sara and she smiles and walks away quickly. She has the same ear tags that I was given. Her tag has the number 322. Indicating to me that she has been here a bit longer than me, and according to my figures, she would have been taken more than 100 people ago. That is a lot. I see only a handful of people like me. I must be missing something. She seems ok though. She is perky and kind. She does turn to look at me a few times as if trying to show interest in talking with me. I am hoping for a chance to use the toilet to get some privacy and motion her.

Wondering when I would get a chance to slip away, I thought maybe it is too soon. I have plenty of time to try to talk to Sara and will just sit content with Stem right now. I am waiting for unanswered questions from him and Barka. The answers are not coming quickly and I do not want to keep repeating myself. Behind me, a young hairy child tugs on my hair. I turn to take a glance at him well and he jolts back like I have scared him somehow.

I whisper to him, "I am Em, do you have a name?" He says in a shy voice, "I am Timber and my sister over there, she is Willow." I smile at him.

He is adorable. He gives me a little pat on the back and runs off. Stem is pleased that the children are accepting me. I know that he is curious about why I have not eaten my mushrooms. I want to show him what the food is like where I am from and am certain that it should have been mentioned previously by someone here.

Surely someone has said before today that this food is primitive and there are other options. He tells me that the meat is from a running whitetail deer. Why running? Is he trying to describe the way that the deer run while he is hunting? Why not make steaks?

"Do you hunt for this up above on your own?" I say.

As I thought again about the meat, "Do you cook this here, or do you have someone else do it?" He smiles and says as his fingers pick at the dried meat, "Come, I will show you."

He stands from his large stump and again takes my hand to lead me away. We wave to all around us and head down a path that I had not been down. This path reminded me of a tiny area that I had explored in as a child. I reminded myself it was too late to take back the questions that I have asked and hesitate to keep moving forward when the path darkens. He does not seem worried about the darkness and with a sharp turn to the left we are standing in an open area that is round like a dome.

Off to the distance I see racks of meat, small fires and smoke tunnels that run sideways instead of up. I am sure that now I know what I have been noticing as an aroma in the air. It was dried meat. I have never seen so much of it. The light from the fires were glowing and casting our shadows on the dirt walls. I noticed in the light that he was actually very man like. He had distinct features. Wide set shoulders and long arms.

"If you are interested in tasting them all, I am working in here next week and will bring you with me." My heart started pounding with excitement that he was giving me information. This helped me understand more about my new life. He said next week. As Barka, had explained, other humans have helped them learn how to account for days and other modern terms. Although, I believe it really means nothing here. There is no urgency to do anything. Life seems the same every day. They need no extras to enjoy their days.

NO money, sugar, soda or milk. What a plan to live by, the nonplan. Just be here and do what you do.

He turned his head to study the rack of meat on the

right side. It was ready and nearby was a large pile of sacks of all sizes. "Stem, does everyone eat the meat at all times, and can they have as much as they want?" His brown eyes looked at me directly and said, "Yes, everyone eats the meat and you may have all that you want."

"I shall take you to see the other areas one day and we shall take the meat with us." he continued. He holds out his hand with a fresh piece and waits for my approval. It is good. I keep some to put in my pocket and feel better knowing that I will always have something to eat while I am here which according to Barka, is forever.

I know deep down, there is a way out. I know that I can find a way to leave or to get help. I have not thoroughly thought that idea through. I will try to take it all in quietly and bide my time here. I demanded to use the toilet quickly as the changes in diet certainly made the urgency come more quickly.

Across from the domed room there was a small place with a crate and lid which is perfect for sitting. It reminded me of the day I was across from Collin and was tagged. I wonder what happened to him as I had not seen him one time since the meeting. There was NO toilet paper and a bucket of leaves nearby.

I quickly grab a leaf and use it the best way possible to wipe the area without obsessing over the fact that this is how all large cases of poison ivy begin. I am trying to understand this way of thinking and so far so good. My mission was complete and I headed back out into the pathway to thank Stem for solving my problem so quickly.

"Stem, I must tell you. I enjoy your company and gift of food and toiletries. I feel guilty in requesting more, but I am hoping there is a way for me to wash my clothing and myself at some point, hopefully without limits." "Please." I add. He responds with a smirk, an extended hand and a "fair enough, I will see that you are cared for." Done.

We walk together back down the pathway, while I hum just a bit. I have always liked doing that and it seemed to make light of the occasion. He seemed to enjoy it as he swung his long arm back and forth a bit to my tune. I have come to realize quickly that the body strength he must have is very intimidating to me. He could forget that I am a scrawny little human and just fling me around accidently.

I will keep that in mind.

Chapter Six

As another week has gone by much faster than I could have ever imagined, Stem is just walking back and forth and stirring the fire. I have not really determined what the fire is for because it is summer and not very cold. Maybe it helps to keep the dampness from the compressed dirt walls. I sleep in my layers and intend to wear the same clothing that I had on yesterday. I stretch and walk over to the fire pit and warm my meat pieces over the coals. He is watching the smoke roll over the meat and squints as I put it to my mouth. "It is not hot, you should try it." I tell him.

I breathe in waiting for his response. Instead of actually saying anything he takes some meat from a sack and puts it on the rocks next to the fire. "Em you are a very good thinker."

I take that as a compliment and we sit down near the fire and eat our blessed meal of, what else, dried running deer meat. It is good and I enjoy it, however I do not enjoy the way that my mouth feels from eating so much of it. The roof of my mouth feels like I have eaten toast over and over. It is rough and I have no way to brush my teeth. There has been no evidence of any type of dental tools. Yet this was another thing to place on the dreaded list. I will bring this up today, because I feel like we are off to a good start.

"I am happy that you do not fear Me." he says. I wait for his next sentence impatiently. "I like having you here and hope that you will continue to be with me."

At that very moment, I took my hand and touched his and said with my meaty smile, "I am happy that you trust me to be here with you."

He then stirred the fire coals once more and stood up, grabbed an empty sack and waved for me to follow him. "Today we will work and deliver the meat to others." He then said something that worried me just a bit, "I will take you and I will guard you." I tilt my head just a little and wonder why he would feel like he needs to guard me.

From what? I stood up and combed through my hair with my fingers. I was used to preparing for my day with a shower and a ponytail. I decided to ask, "At the end of the day is there a place where I can wash or bathe?"

He offered to show me after we were done with our day of working. I walk beside him and imagine all of the work ahead of us. What could possibly be so hard about what type of work he does during the day? I studied his face as we walked and he has a very distinct look with his facial hair just around his mouth and upper lip. It is much lighter and he had a little more red in this area.

He is kind and gentle with his tour giving on our way back to that room. I recognize the area where the crate is for an emergency. I still have not mentioned the leaf thing. For such organized living and perfect English, I am wondering why the modern day amenities are not in place.

His eyes wandered to the walls of dirt as we walked through them. He ran his hand down the sides like a bored child on Sunday. We came upon another male hairy person when approaching the meat room. He said to hello to him. His name was Tangle. Now finally something that makes sense to me. This middle age Sasquatch had the longest of hair and yes, the most matted almost dreadlock hair that could be found here. The humor in hearing his name and meeting him made me smile. He was kind as well and said that the new fires were started and the meat was ready to harvest. I watched them talk for a few minutes and looked ahead to the glow coming from the large domed room. The conversation ended, and Stem said, "This is Em; she is staying with me and is new." I smiled much larger and put my hand out, as my arm was reaching out, Stem took his own hand and put it back down. He held onto my hand and nodded his head. We continued on as Tangle left down the pathway towards the common area.

"You do not want to reach out to others that you do not know; they may take a liking to you and try to obtain your company." I let him know quickly that I understood and that I appreciated his concern. I am relieved to know that he has no intentions of sharing my company. I feel safe with him and Tangle seems a little barbaric and rough around the edges.

"I will show you all that I do, and then you can join in when you want." He said.

I watched him for a moment as we stood inside the room grab a stack of the bags. It is very important to gather the dried meat that has cooled and place the correct amount in the bags. There were three sizes. There were one small brown paper bag size, there was one a bit larger and one that reminded me of a paper grocery sack.

"Deer?" This is from the one that runs fast. "I have never eaten deer before or what others call Venison." I said.

"There are other types of meat. You may find something new after a hunt. We are lucky to have an abundance of this meat." He said.

I was happy to hear that. I was hoping for a nice lean cow next time and trying not to let my thoughts stray at how many other kinds of meat he would hunt for. I followed his lead and the small bags all got 10 pieces of meat about six inches long. They were roughly cut and about two inches wide. I did not mind doing this as it gave me something to do to keep my mind busy. Meat in the bag. Meat in the bag.

I continued until I had a pile of bags finished and he took the small bags that were filled. He put them in the largest sacks. So each large sack was very full of small ones. We continued for about an hour and I asked if I could use the crate. I did not know what to call it, but he seemed to understand what I meant. He walked out into the pathway and just kind of hung out while I went. Oh these lovely leaves of plenty. I was happy to have something but really wished for a cotton towel or napkin.

After finishing up, we went back to the sacks of meat and slid them onto long branches that were all stacked in a pile. He slid them on until the branches were full of sacks and said, "Are you ready to see more of my world?" I accepted his invitation and struggled to carry some to help, which he removed from my hands and smiled.

"I will always carry the sacks."

I follow behind trying to take large steps to keep up with his offer to join him in delivering the finished meat product.

We take the path back to the common place where others are gathered talking and small ones are playing games. We leave no sacks here and continue to the right which was the path we took last time to Barka's office.

The walk feels nice and I look ahead to see what I will discover next. NO way to go up is what I notice most. I keep looking for a ladder or hole showing the sky outside. I remember when I first woke up here there were sky lights or some type of openings with sunlight coming through. I had not seen those in the areas I have been in since the meeting where I met Stem. Others are walking towards us and I am trying not to notice their reaction to me. I am putting everything I can into hoping Stem will realize that I am thankful for his offer to include me and needed the physical release of my energy. As we walk past another male Stem raises his arm to kind of high five him and they both make some kind of noise that sounds like an owl to me. They must be friends.

I do not see any other women or humans like me through the maze of paths that we take. And then suddenly something catches my eye. It is a road sign from up above leaning up against a dirt wall. The sign said Lake of the Ozarks. This area happens to be about an hour west of my town in Missouri. It is a very large area that has many access points so I was not sure if this was something that was brought down to pinpoint the area we were in or if it was just a trinket or souvenir.

The next turn came and after thirty minutes we are in another large common area like the one near Stem's. I smiled as much as I could nervously to show everyone that I was happy to see them. And I really was! There were so many others like myself and more than a dozen other woods people. Stem said nothing for a moment while he stopped to remove some of the sacks from one of his branches. He removed five large sacks that were stuffed to the tops and everyone came to gather them up. This must be how they are distributed to them daily or weekly. I am unsure of the frequency because it was my first day.

I have become frozen in my steps and then step back. My jaws feel like they are trembling from fear and I feel like I cannot swallow. This time as my eyes filled up, I was able to open them widely to look pleased and then looked again at the beautiful woman a few feet away. The tears did not come and I wanted to go back to my cot and forget this day right away. She was about 25 and her tags said 389. She was happy and kind and expecting a baby. I am guessing she was seven months along or so. She collected her sack and went to sit with other females. Some are human some are not.

Now I still think at this present time that some of the Bigfoot or hairy warriors may be part human also. I had really never done my homework on a Sasquatch or Yeti. I know that Bigfoot was seen years ago according to a class I had in school. It was down in Arkansas in the 70's before I was old enough to read. The sightings were of a Beast or Bigfoot. I had seen a gas station when we traveled that way in my teens with a Sasquatch/Bigfoot section that had t-shirts and other memorabilia.

I had never given it another thought. It was not really in my interest maybe because no one in my family that day pointed it out or seemed alarmed. I had no intention of standing there with the meat sacks remembering so long ago. It just sounded so unnatural and yet at the same time very natural. Number 389 walks up and disrupted my thoughts and said in plain English, which was wonderful to hear, that her name is Olive. She is speaking to me and no one is telling her to stop or that it is forbidden so we just continue on. She tells me that she is from Kansas City and is currently mating with Earl. Yes, she just said it. Outloud. She is tagged and mating with a Bigfoot man. I see Earl walk up behind her. It had to be him because she takes his hand and he touches her belly gently. She introduces me to him and he is delightful and kind. He takes the sacks from her and they say farewell and head down a pathway.

Wait! I had so much to say to her! I want to ask her about her life here. I need to know more. Stem notices that I seemed sad that she was gone. He said quietly, "You will see her again. We will always come here to visit and deliver our meats." I felt so happy that he had said that. I needed to be around another woman to feel secure and make sense of all that was happening in the past week or two.

I spun around quickly to follow him and wham, walked right into the branch he was carrying. I felt something wet on my face and my eye closed quickly. I was bleeding and I was able to taste the trickle coming down to my lip. I kept walking and when he turned the corner to make room for me to walk beside him he took notice of my injury.

It was throbbing and he quickly took a look around for something to place there. A crate room was near us and he swept in quickly grabbed a few leaves, and held them to my wound. He then took the strip of vine off of a sack and used it to wrap around my forehead holding the leaves in place. My eyelid or eyebrow felt like it was open and I was concerned.

I nodded to him after he wrapped it and said,"Do you think it is ok?"

He said, "Your outer skin is thin but your inside is strong. You will heal but we will stop and see Barka on our way back." He waved to someone inside the doorway where Olive and Earl were.

Low and behold I see an amazing new hairy male. He is bearing gold locks and a beautiful smile. His hair is not overbearing and somewhat trimmed. It is sheen and it looks like glitter in the light, I am led away after the bags are given to him to finish our work. I asked Stem who that was without sounding too interested and he said Soil, but I knew in my mind, that he was special. I shall call him Sparkle. I giggle to myself and then remember that I am need of medical care and with a swoop and a hug Stem picks me up and continued to carry me down the paths to Barka's office. I can hear his heartbeat and carrying me takes no effort at all for him, his breathe is steady and not animal like at all. There must be some secret to cleanliness I have not been shown yet. My list of questions got larger every moment of the day.

Barka is sitting on a stump drawing on the floor of her office with a stick when we arrive. Just little doodles of a daydreaming Squatch. Good thing I showed up to keep her busy. Stem sets me down on the cot and points to my leafy bandage. "Oh what has happened Em?" she said.

Oh well, "just not paying attention I guess and walked into a big branch." I said. She lifts the leaves off and uses some sort of sponge like material to dab at my eye. I expected some real medical kit to come into play at this moment but I am quickly wiped, blotted and rewrapped with a smile. Hmmm. What a great way to spend the next few days worrying about an infection. At least she did not tie a piece of meat to my face.

"Stem, I want to you to keep this wound clean and bring Em back in a few days if it looks a different color." She ordered. Good advice Barka. I need my eye. I need a ladder. I need my Doctor. Stem thanks her and asks me if I would like him to carry me back. I gladly accept because my legs were tired out a bit and I was hungry.

"Yes, please. May we eat soon and find a crate?" When does he use a crate? Stem is a large being. He must need food and a reason to use the facilities at least ten times a day. He gently picks me up and I know that we are close because of the location we are in.

The commons are empty. There is NO one in sight. I need a clock. It is funny how my time was always so important and that I needed to know every minute what time it is. NO luck here, it is time to be awake. And then it will be time to be asleep. That just about sums it up. Stem carries me behind a large stone wall that is attached to the waterfall and magically what is glistening with beauty is an indoor cave pond. I am gazing at the blue water and gentle steam rising from it. He sets me down on the ledge and with no further a due jumps right in. He goes under then splashes up and really gets a few waves going. There is fresh water falling in and water running out, which somehow must filter this bathing pool. The water is still clear. NO hair. I look at him and take my sweatshirt off. I have little extra clothing and keep that shirt and my shoes to the side. Everything else I wear and am considering hanging to dry overnight for fresh clothing. I slide in the water and while I am enjoying the warm water and beauty, I watch Stem float around a bit and he smiles. When his hair is wet and weighed down I can see his muscle tone and body shape. It is very surprising to me how manlike he is.

He grabs the back of my hair with a tug and splashes water on my back and my head. Careful not to get my eyes wet. He is tending to my needs and I am also really enjoying the atmosphere in this area. It is almost vacation like. I think I am about to turn my lemons into some lemonade.

Chapter Seven

Lying still I open my eyes and drift back off. I open my eyes again and see Stem over by the fire stirring the coals. I feel refreshed from the swim last night and also am happy to have my clothes hanging to dry nearby. I never noticed the way the roots come down into ceiling above me. I am awake now, and so far most of my days just drag on from one to the next. I am thankful over and over again that I am still alive and that I am not starving. I am not excited about the smell of smoke while I sleep and would be really excited to smell something good today. Like laundry detergent or a candle. Something pretty would be nice.

The smoke fogged the room and as the fire started burning more the area became clearer. Not only did the room clear but my mind did as well. I had a clear vision now of what was happening here. Maybe I needed to keep reminding myself because the reality of it was too unreal.

I am trying to change my clothes in the most modest of ways that one can in a large room filled with smoke and a large Bigfoot named Stem. I excuse myself to the small room that has a crate in it and dream of a cup of coffee. I would like to just take it easy for the day and daydream on my cot about life and what is happening around me. As I head towards the fire to sit by Stem he looks at me and says to me that he is sensing that I am worried or afraid. I am not sure how to respond. I want to ask him if I may go home and then on the other hand I am intrigued to find out more about his life. I feel a connection to him. Maybe because he saved me from leaving that meeting with someone that was not as good as him. His eyes look lonely and even though he is very content with his life here he must know there is more. He must know that humans above the ground search for him and his kind and want nothing more than to capture or hunt him down for the big find.

I think about that more and more. All of the years I had seen a Bigfoot toy or sighting on the internet I had really never gave it a second thought. Fear was trying to crawl into my thoughts like a bandit. I was not going to let it win. Once, my mother had told me that we write the story of our life before we are born.

I am now wishing I could call my mother and tell her that I have solid proof that I did not write my book of life. I cannot even envision me back then writing onto the pages that I would get married, have children, get divorced and get kidnapped by a Bigfoot. I am sure she is looking for me. I am sure she is yelling at my ex-husband and blaming him for it all.

I lay my hand over on Stem's hand and ask him what this day has in store for us. Do weekends exist here? I wish it was Sunday. Maybe it is. I have no way of really knowing because there has been no good way to really keep track of my days. He asks me if I would like to go to meet his family. What a coincidence! I was just thinking of mine and now he is offering to share with me his. I thank him and say yes, "Yes Stem, I would really like that." I reach for his stick and poke at the fire. It's not so bad here, at this moment, it is just two beings connecting and it feels safe. It feels almost like home. For a moment.

Stem walks to the other side of the room and gathers up a couple of sacks. We will be taking them meat of course, what a lovely gift. Maybe they are hungry or old. How old is Stem? If I had to guess, I would say very close to my age, but I am probably way off with that guess. For all I know he is a hundred years old or more. He could be younger than me. I have nothing to compare him to as I have only met Barka and the young ones. When we visited the other side, I guessed they must be about my age also. I am excited to find out more.

I stand up as and walk towards the door meeting him and he does a quick wave to send me ahead of him.

Once in the hallway we take a right turn and start walking. I had never been right on this path and am anxiously awaiting the visit we are about to have.

As we walk farther and farther we pass many other rooms similar to his. Open rooms with small fires and trinkets are in sight. Some findings from up above they must be. I saw camping lanterns, a trash can, and even a hammock. Oh those crazy campers, running off leaving their goods just because they heard a noise. Now the source of the noise, if the news caught on would keep people from camping for many years. The people searching for these families are right. The proof is right here walking next to me. One big hairy man. Kind, generous and concerned about feeding others and keeping his fire going. The miles of tunnels and rooms are so massive that I cannot even absorb how big this place must be.

I trip gently on a small rock and stop to pick it up. He makes this noise like a man in the choir clearing his throat. I show him my rock and he reaches out to touch it. "Mmph" he says and does a slight shoulder shrug before handing it back. This was no ordinary rock. It was a jagged little stone with a hole in it from one side to the other. It is a tiny hole. I know from the old stories of hag stones that this rock must have once been in a stream. The running water made this hole through it and so the story goes, they are useful for many things. I would really like to have a book on this to read while I am here. I have seen nothing even close to writing or paper so that may not ever happen. I am surely happy to have this rock. I have an idea. I will work on it later when we arrive back at our room. I slip the stone into my pocket and keep on moving forward. I am really beginning to enjoy these walks. We have walked a long way in the past hour and finally reach a large common area.

As we walk through the entryway, we are greeted quickly with very kind looks and I am very sure at this moment that these others are his family. The females were so kind to come up and touch my hair. The two of them took my hands and summoned me to sit with them while grinning. They looked young but not too young. I still find myself trying to guess ages like I work in a carnival. Step right up; let me guess your age. I think they are all twenty or forty. I just do not know. But then, I see her.

The mother. He takes her gently my way, hand in hand, and presents her to me. The proud neck is showing. She is stunning. She is just a few inches taller than me and her breasts and stomach area are covered with a makeshift braided sack with hair on it. Very nicely done. She takes me in her arms and feels my hair. Her fingers are more bulgy than a human's so they do not go through my hair strands easily. She goes up and down while burying my face in her shoulder of hair.

I reach around and pat her back gently the way I would to any stranger that comes along and feel that this is going very well. She releases me and says that she is very happy to see me. She explains that she had waited many years to see Stem choose his breeder and that I am a good choice.

I fill my eyes again, filling with the small tears that are just a warning of a flood coming. She said that word again. Breeder. Maybe it is just their newly discovered language that is incorrect or it is true that Stem chose me as his future mate. I am sad and unusually unafraid of this. I want to be kind and will not say or do anything to displease him in the presence of his family. He has been kind to me and I feel that tonight when we are back that I may discuss this with him. I have to find the answers that will guide me to a sign of what is next.

My thoughts disappear quickly when I get a glance of the large fire pit across the area and what is on it. It is a large hog, which means pork is cooking. I am the happiest I have been so far to see this. It was something familiar. His sibling placed a beautiful twig crown on my head while walking by and at that moment things could not feel more right. The food and family make it a perfect visit.

As we sit throughout the morning and eat fresh meat while talking about the family, I am feeling good. I am also in need of a crate very badly. I motion for Stem and ask him where the area is to relieve myself and he points in the direction of the room. This one has quite a bit more odor to it and I am sure with this many family members the crate must get used more often by them as well. I go and look around. I use my leaves and feel unusually upset to my stomach. I brush it off and head back out.

This day had me a little more on edge than I had thought and it feels like I just want to lie down. I feel tired. I want to leave.

I sit down and prop my head up against the wall. I sit with my eyes closed just to rest for a moment while they all continue with their gathering. Stem takes notice and all I feel is a touch to my forehead. His large hand gently calls me to open my eyes. I must have fallen asleep for a long period of time. A much needed rest but unusual that I could sleep in this environment.

"We will go now; it has been a long day for us all." He said.

Everyone gathers and waves us off. I still feel tired and he is sensing this. He then picks me up and carries me down the path saving me from dragging my tired legs. I look up and smile. Always giving thanks for the kindness he shows. He has a thoughtful and caring nature which is such a blessing. He does not even struggle to hold me the entire way down the mile long path. It could be longer than that. I keep my head on his shoulder with my eyes closed to avoid an awkward glance. If he thinks I am sleeping it may be easier for both of us.

We enter the doorway to our room and he lays me down on my cot. What a great feeling it is to just rest. I am so glad to just lay here a moment. I hear the fire stir and some clinking around. My stomach feels better and I decide to just fluff up my sweatshirt for a pillow and stay put for a few more minutes.

More clinking around comes from his side of the room. I sit up and look over. He is raising his eyebrows at me while putting some meat on a stick to warm up.

I laugh a little because that meat is by far the best now that I have warmed it. He offers. I snarl a little with no interest at all in meat. He grabs a little sack of the mushrooms and adds them to the stick. I may actually try one of those. The last ones I hid in my pocket and lost. I had always liked the taste of mushrooms. I am still feeling a bit queasy on and off though. I excuse myself to the crate and feel like after a short visit by the fire I may just sleep the rest of my day away.

I sit on the crate and discover the worst thing that could possibly happen at this moment to a female. It was time for my cycle and that explains why I was not feeling my best today. Now what? Leaves? I decide to go against the rules of life and take off my sock; I place it strategically in my underpants and hope for the best. I wonder if I should see Barka. She may be able to help me with something to use.

I head back out to the fire. He looks at me again, and offers me a mushroom. It tastes really bad. I do not want to tell him this but wow, it may be the worst thing I have ever had. I still feel bad and just eat the one to please him, and I am gone.

Chapter Eight

Tossing, turning. Restless. I am not sleeping well. I am dreaming of loud noises. Screaming. Voices. Lights in pathways, running. Whispering. Crying. I am sweaty and looking into the foggy smoke filled room. I do not see Stem by the fire. I look around it is a blur. I see him over in the corner lying in his area. He is sleeping. I do not feel well. I feel drugged. The mushrooms made me sick. I am seeing spots. I see visions of my dreams coming to life. Stem continues to sleep. I drift off again. I dream again, I am being carried. I am scooted down on the flat area that Stem sleeps on and he hovered over me. I felt his breath on neck. I open my eyes and realize that I am dreaming again. I look over and he is still resting.

I find my way to the crate and use my second sock as a way to manage my monthly. I decide to roll up the used sock and quietly go out to the common area to use the water to rinse and clean it. It really is beautiful and it is so quiet. There is no noise or any signs of life. It is just me and the running water. As I turn around and turn the corner I see a large hairy man standing and watching me. He is much taller than Stem and looks a bit older. I am shivering a bit from the sight of him and he is standing in the entryway blocking my way out.

He says, "You have a choice, you do not need to be here with Stem."

I shrug and risk my safety by asking him what he means by that. He leans on the wall and continues to speak.

"You can leave when you find a way and you should be careful. You know why you are here, don't you?" he asks.

I walked towards him a bit more and said in a very quiet voice ,"I am not sure what you mean, I am here because I was trapped and Stem saved me from becoming a worker or maybe even something worse."

"You know that the time is coming soon. You will find out your place here and it will change. You need to go and find your way home. It has never happened before with any of the breeders but it is possible." he continues to say, "If you try hard enough."

"Why not? Why has no one left before?" I whisper.

NO answer. He stands before me and just looks at my face. He starts to move closer and he is struck from behind. He falls to the ground and does not move. I look up to see Stem standing there with a large wood club in his hand. He has beaten this male Bigfoot down and I am not sure if I can look at him for longer than a moment.

"Em, I do not want to do this again, Please do not go alone to any area. I cannot always be there for you." He says and reaches for my hand.

I step over the hair covered leg and follow Stem back to our path. I am sorry and I feel bad. I want nothing more than to go back up above and I now know that no one has ever accomplished that before.

I go to my cot and hang my damp sock up. I watch Stem stir the coals and can tell that he is upset. "Stem, why am I here? And will you please tell me who that was?" I cried a bit to myself while waiting for him to respond.

He says something under his breath and continues in a louder voice, "Our worlds exist together. You are from above and there are no breeders there. Down here under the ground we have lived for many years escaping and hiding from the humans that seek us. I want to say to you that I have chosen you. Because I have chosen you, you are safe from many other things that could have caused harm to you. You have only seen what I have chosen for you to see, and that is the good."

"Why" I stood up. "Why did you choose me? Please tell me what I must do to go back up to the path that brought me here. I will not tell anyone, I promise."

"There is no way Em to ever go back. We have always been superior in many ways to the others that you have known and as our world grows, you will be a part of it. I am happy to have you here with me and you know what your purpose is. It is much the same as mine. I have been chosen to become a breeder as well. For my own kind. I must provide what they are asking for and that is certain."

"Stem, you have said nothing of this before. I hear the words often and one especially and that is breeder. I am here to have children for you?" I feel weak in my legs. I must sit down for a moment.

"When the time is right, you will see Barka and you will produce a child. There have been many successful breeders here and you are looking for answers when the answer has always been there. I do not have the answers to all of your questions in the right way that you want them. I will let you decide. If you would like to provide the child when you are ready or if you would like me to choose the time." he sat down after a short pause and then asked if I was hungry.

"I don't know what this means, but it's no matter. I will do what you feel is best, and continue to be thankful that I am still able to feel safe. I will always want to go home, Stem, I have children there. I will always, miss that." I added.

"Give it time and they may live here too someday soon. You may see each other again." He said.

When the time comes? I will see my family again? I will be a mother to a Bigfoot infant and a breeder. I will be with Stem. I am not sure what will happen next but right now I think I will just warm my meat and sit by the fire. I have no idea again what day it is. I am also unable to determine if we work every day or not. I feel so lost. It is like being camping and having nothing to do because it is raining outside.

I finish my breakfast and visit the crate again. My ear tag is bothering me and I have been fiddling with them when I am alone trying to find a way to loosen them. Stem walks to the edge of the small room and says without looking in, "Your secret is my que to begin. Your mine tonight and I will take you to Barka today to prepare."

I bury my face in my hands quietly crying as hard as I can without making a noise. I just cannot do this anymore. I just cannot. I say nothing and go to my cot. I look up at him with a confused look and lay down with my hoodie over my face. I try to think of happy things in the past. I try to recall some meditating ways to calm myself. I remember a video I had watched once that showed the ocean in the morning with the sun coming up. I tried to pretend I was there. I felt the wind and the sun on my face.

The sound of seagulls and birds filled my head. Oh this is good. I will just stay here just like this for as long as possible and create my own world. One happy world above ground where there is beauty and calm. I turn up the beach waves crashing in my head. It drowns out all of my fears for the moment and my mind quiets down.

As I lay here, I feel so grateful to have had a happy life. I have a very strong sense of escaping this underground Bigfoot Village and I think that the thought of leaving someday will get me through whatever it is I am going through. I am a kidnapped human breeder and am living in a world that no one has ever proven existed. That in itself is enough to take the journey and live to tell the story outside of these dirt walls. I am here, like it or not.

I uncover my head and turn towards the fire. I decided to take out that stone I found during our walk to his families and make him the gift. As I sat up I took off the hemp bracelets and walked over to the stump by the fire. Sitting down next to Stem, I took the rock and unraveled my hemp twine and began wrapping it around the stone. I tied them all end to end to form a necklace. He watched every twist and knot that I made. I took my finished product and stood up next to him to put it over his head. "My gift to you for saving my life." I whispered. He grasped it with his large hand and felt the stone. He lowered it back down on his chest and while it dangled he took my hand. He asked if I was ready to go to the medical area to see Barka. "Yes, if you have decided that this must be done, I am ready." I said.

I catch myself shocked by the strength I just found. I am ok and am going through the motions of what my new life has presented me. I know that it will be a long and trying journey. I am sure at this very moment that I will make it. I stand up once again and take his hand. I am ready to walk the path to see my first friend here and I am actually relieved because I am running out of ideas and socks. I have questions and am anxious and excited to talk with her.

As we walk through the path towards the commons, I pull on Stem's hand so he had to stop, for no reason. Then I walk again. I stop and walk. I was making a game out of our walk together.

At first he looked confused, and by the time we had reached the common area we were jumping ahead of each other and being silly. It was actually really fun. The area was filled with the others and it became quiet as they all stopped to look at us.

Maybe they were all smart enough to build a life for themselves and even learn to speak and elude the best hunters but they never learned to have fun. That side of the brain may not be working yet I am guessing. I keep doing it anyway and laugh at him when he keeps walking without me.

I was looking for that hairy man he knocked out by the water last night and so far I have no clue where he was from or where he could have gone.

Stem slows his steps as we arrive to Barka's area. He became very serious and almost timid. He presented me at the doorway to her and walked away. I was so happy to see her and I knew that there was trust between us from the first day.

"Well, it is good to see you Em, how are you today? Stem had instructions to wait back at his area until you have been informed of your new schedule of events. We will be finished later today. You will be taken back. Are you prepared to begin?" she says as she gets some small crates out from under a cot. She keeps looking through them and I am beginning to think she has lost something. She then steps to the doorway and looks to the right, "Stem, I will see that she is brought back to you at the end of the day, you may go." He did not want to leave. He stood out there even after she had thought he had left. That also pulled at my heartstrings a bit. I feel like he really likes our new friendship.

He looked in as he walked by and glanced at my face. He looked sad. I sometimes think that he is sad a lot but maybe that is just due to the lack of fun around this place.

"Barka, I am doing ok. I do have some questions and am confused about some situations I have come across. First, I am using my socks for this bleeding I am having and I am not sure what the females here do in this situation. The crate rooms only have leaves and I do not have a lot of clothing with me. I am unsure what to do. I am unsure when I can bathe, when I can walk around." I said even more.

"I am not sure what I am doing most of the time unless Stem guides me to the next activity of the day. I would also like to know what day it is and what time it is. I have so many questions. Can you please help me?"

"First things first young lady, you are about to become Stem's partner and now that you will be breeding you will need more information. I am glad to give it to you. In other areas we have classrooms where others like yourself are the teachers and instruct our families how to grow and learn the way that you have up above."

She was still looking through those crates but continued to talk just like nothing was hard for her to say. She explained to me further that I will find out how they track the days and time here and that Stem has a home that he will live in when he reunites with his family someday. Also that where we are staying is simply an area that is set up for him to become familiar with me and my ways.

"Today we will prepare you for your night with him." she reaches out of a crate with a handful of cotton towels. They are like hand towels and seem to be the same sort of lost and found items that I was given before.

"You may use these for your issue, and you may bathe when you like, and when Stem is available to take you. The area that he has been placed in has very few others and it should be easy for you to eat and bathe without too much bother. I was told about your walk out alone and that Broken had found you. He does not think clearly and has been off of his right thoughts for many years." She said.

She was attempting to feel my back and arms while talking now, "Stem will always protect you. It is his job now and as your baby grows he will become more and more devoted and protective. You must abide by this."

Instead of having a complete mental breakdown I allowed her to finish with warm tears in my eyes. They felt warmer than before, maybe because my face felt clammy or damp here. I completed her inspection and followed her lead to the pathway on the right. We walked to a completely new area that was just beautiful. Filled with other females of both Bigfoot type and human. Some blended. As apparently the mix is creating some beautiful short haired versions of me. I am introduced to a group of them and Barka tells them she will be back for me after lunch.

I sit down in the chair that is left open for me and the grooming begins. They stand me upright and we walk around the corner to the most amazing underground cave I had seen yet. Filled with steaming water and so clear I could see clear to the bottom. I stepped up on the stones and we all found a seat together. We floated and swam. We splashed and giggled. I was planning my questions for them as well but they were so carefree, I decided to just enjoy the time and floated towards the waterfall. What a wonderful moment.

As they were mostly undressed with just those small coverings, I decided to take a few items off myself and set them up on the edge. It felt so refreshing and free. I laid back with my head keeping me afloat on the edge of the rocks. Floating away in my thoughts again but this time instead of going to the ocean or going home my thoughts were with Stem. I was becoming anxious as to what was going to become of me and why he really sent me here.

After a few hours of floating, pampering and hanging my clothes to dry we groomed. I was given an unusual style to my hair. This to me looked very cave womanish. I was given the same small fur coverings to wear. These fur coverings are worn by the hairy folks and the humans. Even though they are hairy it seems these coverings must protect their personal and private areas. So whether I am them or not the coverings are to be worn. That bothers me. I love my sweatpants and shirts. I am always cold.

I am wondering where the fur or hair for the coverings comes from. Maybe they harvest it from themselves and wash it before making them. I hope it is not dirty old dusty hair.

I put on my coverings and leave my underpants on. I have to. I have to have some way to wear my cotton towel. I am clean but not soap clean and shaving is not in my future so I can mark off my dream of becoming a hippie child and bask in the beauty of what I have become.

We sit and talk about little things like the water and the others walking around. They are careful not to become privately interested in me or ask questions. I am sure they are instructed to be that way since this must be their job.

A new female comes up. She is human and she is much older. She delivers our meat sacks and I see those little sacks of mushrooms again. NO thank you. Not for this girl today. I felt so bad after eating the last and even though it was short lived, I felt like I was intoxicated. I left them to the side and ate my food. It is the jerky type not the pork kind that we had at Stem's family area. I enjoy my water bottle and even though I still have no clue where they get the water to keep filling them for me I drink it. It is always cold and refreshing. Not from the ponds that I can see, as it would not be as pure. Maybe it was from the waterfalls. I will have to ask. Sometime. But not now as Barka walks in to take me back.

I thank them all, as they wave me off, and walk back to Barka's office. She gets out a sack and fills it with the cotton towels and also gives me another to put my damp clothing in.

"Please listen to me for just a moment Em, tonight you will breed with Stem. You will become as one. You will not experience the act as you have up above. What you call intimacy does not exist here. It is mating in its real and raw form. I wish you the best. I will see you soon for your check up." She smiled and walked me out.

And just like that she looked around the corner and had someone walk me back. A big hairy woman that was kind and stocky in a prison guard sort of way. We walked slowly and I thanked her as we arrived back to my home area. We stopped in the doorway and Stem jumped to his feet by the fire and stared into my eyes. We just stood apart looking at each other. Knowing that tonight was our night to initiate me into his world.

Chapter Nine

He was very quiet and nervous. We spent a while longer looking at each other and he barely moved. His hands were opening and closing and he appeared to be in deep thought. I am sure it was the sight of me in the fur for the first time that kept him looking.

I convinced Stem to sit down by the fire and walked over to him. He touched my hairy coverings and lifted them as if checking the workmanship. His first reaction to my new style was a smile I had not seen before and even though Barka said that this species did not know intimacy, I questioned that. I felt his concern and also his fascination with me.

I touched his hand and as the evening began, I knew that it was close to the time of reckoning. I was not sure what I was supposed to do. Would he kiss me or want to take me to his sleeping area? As he stirred the fire I sat with my thoughts. I was a bit cold. I needed my sweatshirt. It has become a security blanket to me and I wanted it.

Stem took out some meat and warmed it by the fire. As he warmed each piece he fed it to me. An offering I suppose. To show me that he cares for me. I thanked him as usual and asked if he has ever chosen someone before. He looked good. Like he had prepared for this night and he avoided my question. He then said no. I was curious as to why. I was so intrigued by everything that I started to give myself a headache thinking about it. We sat and ate. I tried to tell a funny story about a movie I had seen. I noticed while I was talking that he was looking at the stone on the necklace that I had made for him. I think that he liked it. It meant something to him and that made me happy. I took a drink of my water bottle and swished it around to clean my teeth the best I could.

I liked the flavor of the meat and had noticed that I was losing weight from this diet. Not a lot but enough to notice. I felt healthier.

Stem stood up and held the stone on his necklace in his hand. He took his open hand and reached out for mine. I complied and stood up facing him. As I looked up he bent down and smelled my hair. He smelled my neck and at that moment I felt his hand come up my back and take my hair in his hand. Not forcefully but strong enough to pull my head back while he continued to breathe me in. At that moment I lost myself and allowed him to have his way. I wanted to give him what he waited for.

He took his free arm and hugged the lower part of my back lifting me up to his height. I kept my eyes closed as I felt his breath on my neck and shoulders. His breathing was heavy and he held me tight. He turned around and let me fall to the floor on my feet. I felt the room spin as he stood behind me with his hands on my back walking me forward to the large ledge of his resting spot. My feet were bare and felt roughed up from the dirt under my toes. I dug in as he ripped my coverings off and held my head down on the brown clay colored dirt. At that moment I felt violated and excited at the same time.

As he coasted into me I felt his breathing on my back. As he entered I squinted and held my breath. His interest in me felt like more than just a breeder. We both started to enjoy this feeling and I let him have his moment. I gave him the gift that no one else had given to him.

As his breathing slowed I knew that he was pleased. He backed away and rolled me over while he looked at my face. The look...It is always in his eyes. He moved the hair off of my face and wiped the dirt off. He took my hand and walked me to my cot and said to me that I may change. He did not want to let go, but he did.

I said with a smile, "how about a swim tonight?"

His face filled with joy as he was assured right then that I was not hurt or angry with him. I grabbed my damp clothes and hung them up, and headed to the water area with a burst of energy. It was unusual and frightening. It was exciting and different. So many different feelings were inside of me and to honest with myself, I had not felt this alive in a very long time.

I dove into the water the best that I could considering the depth. I splashed him and floated by. I soaked and relaxed. I enjoyed the feeling of the warm water on me. It was a nice day and a thrilling evening filled with feelings I have never known. I swam to him and held the rock around his neck.

And then I said, "Thank you Stem, for caring for me."

He said in return, "Tonight I must hunt. It is tradition to mark the day of my new life. I will hunt and return by sun up above ground while you rest."

That made me worry a bit with Broken the Bigfoot man around I was scared to sleep on my own. I wanted to tell him that but before I got the chance to, as we walked back to our area, his parents were inside waiting by the fire.

"They will stay with you while I hunt. You will be safe."

Chapter Ten

I felt relieved and I felt shy. His father was covered in gray hair and his mother had such a kind personality but was definitely older and needed rest. I nodded to him and thanked them for coming. They went to rest in his area while he gathered his sacks. He stirred the fire one last time and left for the path.

I was so happy to go to the crate, and get my warm clothes on. I had my cotton towels and had such an eventful day that I knew I would rest well. I laid there thinking about life again. I could not help it. My mind was just so busy with thoughts. I had fallen asleep content, knowing that all is well, right this moment. All is well.

Dreaming with visions of Stem up above in the forest hunting. I am not sure if where I am is very close to the woods that were near my house. I see him walking through the leaves and tall weeds. I see him looking for a deer or wild boar. I wondered what he would actually use to kill his prey. Would it just be with his bare hands?

The fire flame went out and it was enough smoke to wake me from my dream. I sat up on my cot and seen Stem's family sleeping and walked over to the fire to stir it a bit to get the red coals together enough to blow on it. That always seems to work to get a little flame. It is actually nice to have him away for a moment so I can feel in charge. Not that he is very controlling but I love playing with fire. I will make use of my time alone and head to the crate. I am also going to go out and wash up even though I was advised against it because of Broken Bigfoot. I have not seen him again and he must just wander from common area to common area.

Yes I will take a quick swim. And a wash of my clothes to hang up will be nice. I will feel in order for the first time since I have been here. I am a bit disturbed and intrigued at the same time about the relations we had last night.

It was actually very exciting and he is actually a very kind and caring man. I am not sure why my path in life led me in this direction but I am making the best of it until I know how to change the situation.

I want to go home and then on the other hand I am happy to feel like my own person. I have lost that feeling for many years being a wife and mother. Everything I did was always about them and never for just me. I am not complaining. I am just being honest with myself. I was in a very rigid daily routine of motherhood and it was to the point where I literally was just a maid, just a driver, just a provider.

No one ever took the time to ask me about me. I guess that is why I enjoyed my walks so much alone. I do miss my dog. I did miss her the most out of everything that I left behind besides my family. I know that sounded cruel but it is how I felt.

I headed to the water and looked around carefully. At the far end that female that I had met long ago was here. Mary was sweeping the table area with a large branched broom. It looked much like the old witch brooms I had seen on display at Halloween shops. She was cleaning and gave a wave. I felt comfortable knowing she was nearby. I jumped in the water and splashed around. I rinsed my clothing out. I had plenty of the cotton towels left and this would give me a new stack of clean ones.

I had some marks on me from Stem. Just small burn like areas maybe from his hair rubbing me. It is almost like a carpet burn. I want to trim his hair and brush it. That sounds crazy but I do. It is very fine and not crazy at all. The thickness is just right and I can see now how it must protect him while being up above. His long arms and muscular body has a cover in brown hair with a reddish blonde tinge. I have seen others with darker hair and some more red in the corridors. What I really liked about Stem's appearance was his facial features. The sides of his face had shorter hair like a beard. Setting off his smile and big brown eyes.

I am sure that I am missing some information when it comes to their self-care. Like how they live in certain ways. I am not seeing what I believe is happening around here. I know there must be a way that they are taking care of their teeth and their bodies. It is too obvious to me. Only because there is not a lot of foul odor. There is some but not as much as you would think.

It is natural and sweaty but not dirty or foul. I am hoping to discover their secrets so I may get out of that dirt room and be able to feel more comfortable.

My swim is over and I gather up my wet items to take back with me. Mary is still across the room and it is quiet. I am guessing it is about 5am but really that is just a guess. I will hang my clothes and warm some meat. If the family still continues to sleep I may lay back down for a bit. I am not sure how long Stem will be away. How did he get up there? There must be a way nearby and there must be a way to actually get what he has hunted down here easily. I can see though that the same type well that I fell into would easily trap animals. That is an excellent plan on their part. Maybe it was for animals and I just happened along at the wrong time.

The sack was filled with new meat and I grabbed just a few to warm up. The fire coals were warm and felt good. It was still comforting to just sit and relax without a lot of stress and worry about what is happening around me. I think that it will be a good day. I am happy to be safe and taken care of in such a kind way.

While resting on my cot with my warm hoodie I sense something.

Above ground, Stem is hurdling through the thick woods with his kill.

He has spent several hours tracking down a whitetail doe and a buck. As he traveled through the weeds and stomped through the mud he stopped to listen carefully to noises around him.

He moves swiftly and drops off his prey near the area that he uses to access our underground village. He takes special notice to campers and tents. This is usually the best way to carefully pick up a few desired items.

He collected a few stainless steel marshmallow sticks and a small cooking grate off the fire top. Also there was a beautiful oil lantern. He is careful not to alarm anyone or make his presence known. I see him in my thoughts walking through the streams and hills to find his way home.

I had only heard a few stories in my lifetime of the Bigfoot and other species that is similar. Not one time had I ever heard that one had been captured, harmed or killed.

I know there must have been thousands of sightings over the years in the states surrounding Missouri and here I was smack in the middle of the best evidence anyone could ever find.

Bigfoot exists and there may be thousands, even though, I have only seen less than 30 or so. I am sure that there is many more. They must be quick and elusive. The power they have physically allows them to make it home safely and without harm.

I wonder if there are traps out in the forests and woods that humans have made to attempt to capture them. I had only seen news stories that would show people in the woods looking for them and it was always at night. Most sightings must be at night however most photos I have seen were always in daylight.

I am anxious to know the details of every question I have in my mind. I am now living in a new world and am adapting quickly. I am torn between trying to accept this new relationship and being titled a breeder. And also wanting to get out of here immediately. I feel like I may be losing my mind. I may not be ok.

I snuggle on my cot with my eyes closed and hear Stem's parents wake up and head to the hallway. They know the secret of avoiding my crate area. I wish I knew where they were going. I am just going to stay right here. I am emotionally and physically drained.

I hear commotion in the hallway. It sounds like many others coming down the paths. I continue to lay still and not look at them directly as they walk by. There is a group of more than 10 so far. They were shaking the walls from the weight of their footsteps.

Suddenly I hear Stems voice. He has returned! I hear everyone cheering and making loud noises to greet each other. He has returned from his hunting trip which was a celebration of our time together. I have not thought too much of that for most of the night and am curious to know if it will happen again.

It was a quick trip. It was only one night. Stem showed up in the doorway and I greeted him with a smile. His family had not really said much to me and that is ok. They just are not that way.

It was not until he left that I actually thought of him

much. And now seeing him kind of makes me happy. I am sure he is happy to see me as well and he heads over to the fire pit to place the newly found items that he gathered during his trip. He then walks up to me and with a kind and caring voice he said "Em I am glad to see you, I thought of you while I was away and I found a gift for you."

I was like a little kid on Christmas morning at that point. I wonder what it could be. I stood before him and squeezed my eyes shut as tightly as I could. Holding out my hands while saying READY! I felt him whisk by and because of his size the breeze tells me he went to the pathway.

One moment later I am tempted to peek but keep my patience and soon I feel him place something very large and heavy on my hands. It feels like a belt or a strap. I open my eyes and I am staring at the strap of a huge duffel bag. Not just a small or medium but extra-large! It is packed full and covered in dirt. He must have drug it through the woods for many hours.

"I found this up above. I hope that it will make your day good." He said.

Dragging over to my cot, I am having visions of being home again with the feeling of new stuff after a shopping trip. Could I really find some joy in this bag?

He spent some time over by the fire with his new items and worked on the fire while looking over at me with the eyebrow raising thought of why I had not opened it yet. I smiled and grabbed that big zipper and opened the bag. The bag was filled with clothing, shampoo and soap! There was unopened toothbrushes and toothpaste! Digging in further I had found deodorant, a hairbrush, socks, playing cards, a coffee mug and a bag of coffee. There was so many treasures in this bag that I was brought to tears to see it all.

I knew that some of the things were used and old, but I had no need to worry about that. I could tell by the Cabela's bag that the person who had owned this had great shopping taste. I wonder who she was. I wonder if he went near a campground or some campers out in the woods. I wish there was another bag filled with something for him. I am sure he can have all of the bags that he would like but has no use for them.

The simple life requires no extra fun. I know that he may enjoy some of these items. I am going to search for something to make some coffee over that fire if it is the last thing I do.

I am also going to take that soap with me to the water tonight, if he is around and wants to go. I am wondering if he will be going again soon? How often do they hunt and travel? I know it must be a huge risk to go to an area where this bag may have been. I am thankful for it.

I take my brush and go sit by him at the fire. I brush my hair a bit and then take his hand to show him how it feels afterwards. My hair is so oily and straight. Washing it in the water helps but it does not really get it clean. I am going to scrub up and my thoughts are bouncing around in my head creating ideas of what fun it will be. Maybe he will let me show him how to use this stuff.

I feel like he will try something new if I show him how amazing it is. The comforts of life are a reality today. I could not be happier than I was right at this moment. I thought about the busy world up above and wondered what everyone was doing. I am becoming one with this life now because I needed to for survival reasons. I am not sure that I can even call home my home anymore. It was where I lived. It was where my happiness was. It was gone in one moment. The moment I fell into that well.

Fate? I do not know. There must be a reason for everything. I thank Stem and walk bag over to my big bag of coolness. I think I will just sit here and dig through the clothing and little pockets. Maybe there are some little treasures I have not located yet.

Sure enough there it was. A small zip pocket with a necklace and a watch. A watch! It says 9:00. I know that it is morning and I have a watch! Whew! I threw my hands in the air with happiness. I can tell time in this crazy time free under the woods zone.

I am ready to put this on and I hope that it last forever. It is not a dainty watch. It looks like a man's watch for hunting and it has a lot of buttons. I am tempted to press all of them and the smart part of my brain tells me to make the battery last. However long that could be.

I wrap it around my wrist and put it on the last hole. I look through the back of the bag and find some energy bars. And also a chocolate bar. I feel faint. The happiness is now overwhelming and I make a decision to stop until later in the day to simmer down and get my day started.

As Stem warms some meat, he extends his hand out with some for me. I am goofy and standing in front of him with my cup and new bag of coffee. I hand him the foil bag and he smells it. The aroma is wonderful. I take my water bottle and search around for a way to heat the water. I am thinking that a piece of fabric may make a filter. I will work on that another time. It seems that he is tired and needs rest. I wave him over to his area and touch the stone on the necklace that I made for him. He touches my hair and turns to go and lay down.

"I will just rest for a while, and you can do what you like. Please do not go too far I must be sure you are safe." He said.

I grin and say, "I will stay close." and run back to my bag to start sorting out the items. What a great morning at home. My new home. My underground Bigfoot filled home.

Chapter Eleven

I had never felt so happy in the past few weeks as the moment that this big old duffel bag appeared to me as a gift. I was thrilled to have the treasures that I had found. Just the first few items were such a thrill and then to discover there was even more in small pockets and zipper bags was a wonderful surprise. I was looking forward to my swim tonight and was waiting patiently for Stem to wake up.

I lay back down on my cot with my new items and thought about what kind of person owned all of this. I wonder if it was a married couple and they spent their weekends camping. Maybe they were Sasquatch hunting? Were they spending their time looking for this bag? I envision Stem trolling the area and taking the bag when no one was looking. I bet they believe in Bigfoot now if they got a glimpse of him in the area. People will think they are crazy if they tell the story.

I laid out my warm comfortable clothes and the soap I wanted to take with me. I even have a beach towel now. Counting the hours or minutes on my new watch until he opens his eyes. The comforts of life were certainly right before me.

I lie quietly for a few minutes and hear Stem wake up. He smells like fall leaves from his trip. I would love to smell fresh air and see sunshine again.

Suddenly I hear commotion from the common area and he jumps to his feet with a loud landing and tells me to stay still. A group of large hairy men stand at the doorway and he uses his arms to keep them from coming into our area. I hear them talk but cannot make out the words.

They look angry and he walks towards them gathering them to try to get them to walk down the pathway to talk to him away from where I am. I take this opportunity to go to the crate and plan to stay in there as long as I can.

I am feeling nervous and I am not sure what is happening. I hear crying and screaming. It sounds female. It sounds like a female human. I hear her voice.

Then, there is nothing. Just silence. I hear no sounds. I look at my watch and it says 3pm. It is time for nothing because nothing ever happens around here. There is nothing to plan and we just eat when we are hungry and sleep when we want. I am undecided on whether I should go back out to my cot. I know Stem will try to keep me safe and keep me out of the trouble that has brewed out there. It just seems odd.

I feel a large hand reach around the corner and grab my neck. It is squeezing and I am gasping for air while trying to stand up to get away. I am screaming for Stem with the little voice that I have left and something is stuffed into my mouth. I feel a large cloth or sack placed over my head and my hands are held behind my back. I am in danger and he promised to protect me.

The large Bigfoot man picks me up and I feel the hair of his arm on mine. I am thrown over his shoulder and held tight. I am running out of air and I feel dizzy. I feel a panic attack. I am scared.

We are running. Running a long way and he has me on his shoulder. I am getting the breath knocked out me and am too far gone to try to fight and run. I cannot see where I am or where we are going. Slam. I land on the ground and lay still Crying. I get my hand on the sack enough to pull out what was in my mouth and stay silent.

The man that has done this to me places my hands together once again and wraps the familiar earthy vines around my wrists. I now sit with my back in a corner. I feel the dirt through the back of my shirt. It is cold and chills me. He leaves me behind and I sit alone and taken. I am away from my area and this is not a kind act. My watch is hurting me and the vines are tight.

He has left and I am sitting in the dirt without one of my shoes and my hands tied behind my back. I close my eyes and am grateful that the sack on my head is easy to breathe through and is keeping my face warm from the air I am breathing in and out. I will just drift off in my thoughts and ease my mind. I am worried about Stem.

I am afraid that those hairy men hurt him. What went wrong? Why would they do this? Who was that woman that I heard screaming?

I see the woods in my dream. I reenact my walk through the paths that led me here. I had been there many times and I believe I have been here about a month or so. I see the woods filled with police crime tape and a sign that has been put up to keep others from using the area.

The news stories on TV are updated every night with my photo. I am missing. I have been searched for by hundreds of local volunteers and my family. There has been no hope left for them to find me alive. But I am. I am here. I have been bred. I have been kidnapped. I have been bound and tied from the only place I felt safe while I was here.

It has been a few hours and I still hear nothing. I see no light. I see no signs of life around me at all. I have no water or food. I have no crate. No shoe.

I drift away to sleep because I do not know what else to do. I cannot get warm. So I just rest.

In the morning hours I hear noise and there is the feeling of someone in the room with me.

"Is someone there? Please tell me if you are?"

A voice that is familiar to me says, "I am here and I did not bring you to this place. How did you get this far away from Stem?"

"Please help me, I was taken here and I need air. I need water. If you know Stem can you take this sack off of my head and take me back to him?" I said crying. "Please!"

"I cannot take you back. I can take the sack off and get you water. I can find Stem and I can tell him that I had seen you. It may help him to befriend me again." He said. "Let me help get those off of your hands." The vines were untightened and I wiggled my hands out of them after they were loose enough.

I looked at him when I removed the sack with my free hands and it was Broken! The same Bigfoot that Stem had to club down is the same one that is trying to save me.

"Will you take me with you, to find Stem?" I said.

"I cannot take you if someone was to see me with you it would cause a bigger problem. I am not sure who brought you here. I will be careful to get back the message of where you are." He said, as he handed me a small bag of water. It was similar to a metal flask only leather. It was a pouch of some sort. It really made me sick to stomach to think that he drank out of it also. I looked around the room to make some type of plan to escape.

I was relieved to have water and as he left I felt the warm sensation of my own urine coming. I had nowhere to go.

My sensitivity kept me proving to myself that I was alive. I had given my all to satisfy my new life and was left with no other options. The mess I was in was so horrifying that I did not know if I could make it another day like this. I had to find a way to leave. I wish he would have taken me with him. With the sack off it was easy to see what was around me and that was nothing. There was nothing around me. It was just an empty room.

The light was starting to peek in a little as the day started. I had spent the entire night dozing on and off. I was not tired physically but mentally exhausted. There was no law or order here that I could see. I was fine and then not fine. The men that were angry and that were involved in my kidnapping would be high on my list of who I would want to never see again. I do however want to see Stem. I really missed the feeling of being taken care of. I thought about his eyes and the sadness that must be in them.

As I sat in the corner with wet pants and tears on my face I knew I must face my fear of what could be out there and at least look. Just once. I scooted across the room about 8 feet to look outside. I had seen an empty common area. It all looked unused and abandoned. Almost like it had not been touched for many years. I also had seen what looked like a door. A real square of stone and wood planks that could open up. Maybe into a fire pit or maybe it was to the outside.

As I took off the last of the vine on my wrist I grabbed it and put it in the sack that was over my head before. I also put in my water. I had nothing else. Except my watch and it was dirty and cloudy under the glass.

I must have damaged the watch when I fell onto the floor. Maybe it was when I was taken. I continued to look around and back and forth as quickly as I could.

It was almost like crossing a busy road.

My head was just paranoid and I could not take a stop without listening for a noise. I made it over to the hatch door and was able to open it. It slid right open. It was filled with leaves and sticks. It was filled with spiders and water. It looked like the bottom of a well. It was very similar to the well that I had fallen into but older. I knew it was not the same one because I was captured near the medical area. There were cots and other humans where I was before.

Here there was no sign of anyone. Bigfoot or human. No noise, any smoke or fire areas. There was not one thing to recognize. I tried to move some of the leafage away from the doorway carefully without letting it all spill out. I was sure I could fit through the hatch and I wanted to see if there was light up above. Sure enough I could see a ray of sun. Not a lot of light or sun but enough to know that this may be a way out.

Just as I had moved enough to climb in I heard voices. I heard pounding. Maybe it was my heart. It was a group of men. They were very loud. I slid into the rock well and pulled the trap door closed behind me. I was panicking at the thought of insects and the unknown touching me or biting me. I listened carefully and heard yelling. I know that the man who had taken me was out there. He had seen that I was gone. He was angry.

He was with others and they must be some type of group that is out of control or not a part of the good community down here. It was some sort of bad boy club. I stayed put. I was careful not to move. I was not leaving this hatch unless I heard Stems voice. I knew that it was a long shot that Broken could get a message back to him.

It was possible though. If he was trying to get back in the good graces of Stem that this may be the best way to do it. I wanted to dig through this mess of forest trash and stand up but was afraid to move. I decided to move over away from the hatch and cover myself with the leaves in case I was discovered. I felt safe.

I laid there just breathing and looking up at the sun beam. The hole was mostly covered and about 6 foot wide. There was just enough to see the outside.

I could wait all day and try at dark to climb this rock wall. There was not much texture to it. Very much like the other one with moss and very slick. I am not sure that night would be better considering that is when I know that they hunt. It may be best to just wait until the end of the day before dark and see what I am capable of coming up with. I have no idea what I am doing. I am really just a mess at this point. I have no real plan. I have really just had enough. I felt depressed and sad. I felt like maybe this well was the last time I would see sunlight. Maybe it would be the last time that I breathe.

I felt bugs crawling. I had seen a mosquito. Please keep me safe. I thought to myself over and over. Please let this end well. I could not hear anything outside of the small door. The sound was gone. It was barricaded by the wood planks. If something was going on I could not hear it.

I stayed still. I wanted to move and test the rock wall to see if I would be able to climb. The sticks were not big enough to stand on or escape with. I could not yell for help with the hopes of someone passing by. I had no idea where I was even located. I did not even know if it was the same wooded area I fell into originally.

I checked my watch. It said 11am. It would be a long day. Sleeping was always my cure because it passes time and helps me think. I had to think. I had to find a way to do something or just give up.

Hours passed by and still nothing. There was nothing at the hatch. There was nothing at the top. I was getting covered in bug bites. Small bugs were biting my ankles and legs. I noticed a tick on my arm and flicked it off. I pulled the sack up to chest level and took out my water. There was not a lot in there but it was enough to keep me going for a few more hours. I drank about an inch of it and decided to save what was left.

I pulled my sleeves down over my hands and tried to cover any exposed skin that I could. My body hurt. I had changed my physical routine and felt stiff and sore. I became a breeder and let my body become physically used by a Bigfoot. I was taken and thrown by another and now lay in the raw mess of this new life that was given to me.

The hatch opens. I start to shake a little. I have no tears left. I am hungry and dehydrated. I lay as still as possible while I feel a hand near my feet checking the leaves. I heard no voice and there was no way to tell who it was without speaking out. So I continued to lay motionless. Go away. Please. Go away. And then I heard out in the room a voice. While the hatch was still open I heard it again. It was Broken's voice. He was telling someone that he had seen me.

"She was right here, in this room over here. She was there and I helped her." he said.

And then I heard the sweetest grumble. It was Stem.

He was there and I was undecided what to do. I could announce myself. I could have a chance to go back safely with him. Or I could lay here and try to get out. I was torn. I was making bad decisions. I was questioning myself.

I decided to do what I thought was best and with tears in my eyes I sat up and said, "I am here, please help me."

Stem ran to the opening and cleared the leaves so quickly with his big arms. He took hold of my feet and pulled me to the hatch. He then picked me up while I cried hysterically and he held me. He held me tight. He rocked me and let me cry. I was so grateful for his kind spirit and the feeling of his kindness filled me with warmness. I could not let go. I grabbed hold of the stone necklace and held it tightly in my hand. I thanked Broken and told Stem that without him I would not have been ok.

They walked together down the pathways and we never encountered anyone. No noises and no other Bigfoot. We walked quickly and Stem thanked Broken as we arrived at our area.

He then left while Stem carried me to the fire area. He sat down with me and did not let me go. I did not want him to. I was itchy and scratched up. I was dirty and covered in insect bites. I needed water and food. I told him everything and he said that we would be leaving to stay now with his family in our own area. It was an area that would always feel safe.

I was ok with that and hoped that we would be leaving soon. He moved my hair away from my face and said it was time to go. At that moment his father was in the doorway. He helped me pack my duffel and treasures. I made one last trip to my crate room before we left and recovered my shoe. With everything ready to go Stem picked me up once more to help me stand and we went together to the right. Towards his family home. We were going home.

Upon arrival to his parent's common area many came to greet us. We were smothered with love and a welcome feeling. It was very much needed for me to feel ok again. Stem told me that we would all be leaving together. This area was a temporary stay for his family as well as a sacrifice for his new life. His new life was finding me. They all gathered belongings and he set me down gently on my feet to help collect sacks and items to carry off.

We all grouped together and started walking to the right. A new path I had never traveled. It would lead us far away from my old home and all that was familiar to me.

We traveled for more than two hours until we came upon a small opening. As we traveled I pretended to hear background music. It was traveling music with a light guitar sound.

The opening looked just like one of the other very small dirt rooms and there was a room that looked like a crate area. We went in and there was a doorway that was hidden to another path. It was a maze of paths and as we went further down the mulched walkway we approached what was the most beautiful home I had ever seen. It was a doorway that was castle like. It must have been more than thirty feet tall. It was surrounded by broken and staggered twisted trees and rock walls. It was an underground cave with a warm feeling to it. Just outside of the doorway stood two Bigfoot types as guards.

They welcomed us home and as we entered I was speechless. I had my mouth open and eyes large at what was before me. It was almost a real home. It had a real fireplace and a real living area. There was a large fire stove and dishes. There were blankets and lanterns and wooden furniture pieces. It was beautiful. Off to the side on the left were many large rooms for sleeping and he took my hand and led me to ours.

The room had a large cot for me and many human made items. There were lanterns and matches. There were camping supplies and garden tools.

I also seen many items displayed and it must have taken many hunting trips to collect this many over the years. I was in awe. Stem set my duffel bag down by the cot and pointed to the crate room that was just ours. He had a large slab in the corner to sleep on.

I felt like I had always said thank you so much that it was losing value. I walked over to him and put my head on his chest. He ran his hand on the back of my head and asked if I would like to go to the water to clean up and talk. I was happy to hear that. I wanted to talk to him about what had happened. I also wanted to use my new soap and get some clean clothes.

He asked me to get what I needed. He grabbed an empty sack and led me out by my hand. We walked to the back of the cave and behind the stone was an underground pool of beautiful steaming water. It was larger than any swimming pool I had ever seen. There were more seats here and towels! This really was an amazing place and although it was primitive it was very nice. Very modern compared to what I have seen since I have been here.

I sat on the edge of the water and scratched my ankles and legs. He looked at the bites and then with the touch of his thumbnail pulled a tick off my neck. I had so many open areas and scratches. His nails were very similar to mine. They were more round and very thick.

I walked into the water and rubbed my bar of soap on my arms and face. It smelled so good. It was taking me back to the days when I was very young and we had a bath at grandmas. The soap smell was familiar. I had never really used bar soap at my home. Everything was bottled. I scrubbed and washed.

I swam for a few minutes and waded up to him on the ledge. I took his hand and rubbed some soap on it. He had that funny look that always caused his eyebrows to rise up. He smelled his hands and I washed him some more. We started wading and washing and the company was good. We had similar souls and we had bonded.

It was so amazing that I could have just stayed all evening. I knew we had to eat and rest. I really needed to do that after what had happened. I asked him about that and he said we would talk more about this but those men were bad and they spend most of their time hurting others and also collect breeders. He said that I was lucky to ever see him again. He was happy it worked

out the way that it did and it will never be that way
again. He promised.

I grabbed a towel and rubbed my hair. I wrapped it
around me. I had left my clothes on just mostly due to
modesty and also to clean them. I wanted to wash them
with the shampoo. Another day. For right now meat
and bed sounds good. A blanket sounds really good. I
remembered that there was alcohol wipes in that bag
and it was the perfect solution to my itching areas. I was
miserable and tired.

I peeled off my wet clothes and placed them in the
empty sack he had brought along. I stood there for a
moment just looking at the water. I looked at Stem as
he dried off and looked at me.

Wearing only my towel and underclothes he walked
up behind me and touched my back. His hand moved
up and down it like a paintbrush making art. Suddenly
his hand went up under my wet hair and once again he
took it into his fist. He held it tight and smelled the
back of my neck.

I was pressed forward on the ledge and the force of
him was so great that I broke my fingernail grabbing the
stone around me.

He took me again to his world without notice and I lay on the towel covered rock shivering. Not from the cold but from his passion. It was real and I felt it.

Taking my hand as usual, I was helped to my feet and I felt weak. We walked to the kitchen area and ate together before going to our room. The amount that he eats compared to mine is incredible. I had never really noticed the amount of calories he must require for his size. Laughing and talking. It was a night I would never forget. Again.

Chapter Twelve

The morning came quickly and I slept very well with my new found comfort. I loved the feeling of being warm. It was not cold here but just lacking in warmth. I decided to find a way to make that coffee today. Even though there was no milk I just wanted to smell it. It was a smell that I used to love so much in the mornings.

"My parents are leaving for a long trip to see others and I do not want you to be afraid. I will be leaving tonight to hunt and you will be well guarded." He says to me as soon as he sees my eyes open.

I said, "That is a lot of news for one girl that just woke up." He knew I was joking somehow and smiled.

I was ok with being alone for a while if it was safe. I could make my coffee and swim. I could just be me for a while and dream of the days behind me that were normal and sunny.

"They are leaving now, so please do what you would like. I will be preparing for my trip and will tell you when it is time for me to go." And just like that he grabbed a handful of sacks and touched my face as he walked towards the door.

I thought about what it was like for him up above. I wondered if he became frightened. I feel worried about him now and would be devastated if anything ever happened to him.

I spent most of the day puttering around looking at things. I peeked in the other rooms and at the items that were stacked in corners and placed on ledges. I could tell that almost everything they had was either from old farms or campgrounds. No evidence anywhere that they had been to a big city or large store.

And then, my eyes feel huge. I am in awe of what I see while looking in a large sack. Cans of soda! Well who knows how old they could be but they look fairly new. The types of brand labels are all modern so they must not be too old. Glaring at the numbers was not as easy as the light is very dim. The light here never seems bright enough for my taste. I would really love to have big bright lights. The glow here is similar to a candle. I go for my duffel to dig for that little flashlight I had seen. The numbers are all in red and even though I cannot make out the month it is definitely this year so I crack one open.

It is warm but the can is cool on the outside from the air down here. It is bubbly and tasty. This is going to be a great day I can feel it. I found an old blanket and laid it out on the floor by the fire to dump out my bag.

I wanted to lay out everything that was in there and really go through it now that I had some time alone. Right after I have some crate time and some granola from the bag. Oh my taste buds are in heaven right now.

I carefully laid out all of the socks and shirts. Granola bars. Popcorn!
Markers, notebook, baby wipes. Alcohol wipes.
Bandages. Insect spray. Hair ties.
A bracelet. Tweezers. Roll on Deodorant. Lotion.
Another bar soap. Nail Clippers.

Now for the exciting stash, the little zipper pockets. A map of Arkansas? Odd.
Headache medicine, a dollar bill! Toothpaste, toothbrush. Used. I am still happy with that.

Another pocket. Nothing. Last pocket. Chocolate! And a peppermint.

I am happy to have every single item I have found. I am also grateful for the female products I found.

I really have no use for the dollar bill but everything else is wonderful! I spent some time placing it all back in neatly and wonder around for a place to brush my teeth. I am doing it. I do not mind that it belonged to someone else. I could boil some water in something over the fire and it would be good as new. I am tired of being afraid. Tired of looking to the days in the past when I was paranoid of germs and being so perfect.

This new life has really changed my perspective so much. I always felt disappointed in myself and unaccomplished. Here I feel like I am proud to be me. I was the survivor and the woman who never really got to be who she wanted to be. So then I fell in a hole and changed the world. Ok that may be a little over the top. I did feel proud though to be able to get through this day to day.

I sat back on my cot and put my sweatshirt over my head. I wanted to throw the blanket over but it seemed dusty to me. I will take it with me to the water today and wash it. For now I will just lay here. I just want to sleep the morning away with my belly full of soda and granola. I will just rest.

Stretching and falling back asleep a few times does feel nice sometimes. If I compare it to my old life of alarm clocks and schedules it is certainly more relaxing and stress free. I am less stressed since I stopped needing answers to the hundreds of questions I created after arriving. Now that it has been a month or more it is hard to remember what it was really like at home anymore. I remember it but it does not feel real. This feels real.

I rubbed my eyes and went through my hair with my fingers still checking for old bugs. I grabbed my things and that big dirty blanket and headed for the swimming hole. It was lit so beautifully with the lanterns and I grabbed a couple of towels to lie on the rock ledge. I wanted to wash everything with my new shampoo and was certain that I would regret it later. I knew I needed it to last for say, the next twenty years.

I sure hope not. I hope that I only need this shampoo for another day or week. Not for a year or two or ten. I washed out the blanket first and hung it over a big rock.

I was hoping it would dry before nightfall. I washed out a few more clothing items and laid them out and swam away. I floated and washed. I really enjoyed the moment of swimming undressed and not watched. It was just me and my soap. It was just me and my steaming water.

I am at the end of my internship here. I am not new anymore and have learned so much more about the Bigfoot ways. I am sure that how it is today is how most of my days are just going to be. I was sleeping, swimming, discovering, and waiting for Stem while he hunts. I wonder since it was still morning when he left if he was meeting others and preparing to go out or if he was going to be going alone.

I see him going up and walking through the trails. I see him searching for his kill while he marks his areas by ripping branches down as he goes. As he kills one deer with his bare hands and delivers it to a well to be taken in by workers, he continues to look for more food. He walks for miles to areas familiar to him and some new. He was looking for trinkets and goodies. Exploring and stalking the woods while avoiding and hiding from hunters or people nearby.

Stem was making swift and smooth strides through the trees. He was checking traps and areas for other prey. I admire the determination and strength to keep going for so many hours without sleep. .

I checked the kitchen for a meat sack and could not believe that I was actually hungry for it. I could see out towards the big entry way that the guards were still there.

They were drinking water and talking in calm voices. I could not tell if they were the same ones that were there when we arrived. I see some differences in the ones that I have met and talked to and if I have not had that chance they all kind of blend in. A lot of similar features and the biggest difference is facial hair, hair colors and hair length. Mostly all that I have seen have big brown eyes. He had caring and non-judging eyes. Sad and devoted eyes.

After hours of exploring the area, swimming and eating I had finally decided to rest.

It was quiet but the noise of the water area was soothing. Like a stream with a little noise to drown out the eerie silence. It was also the kind of noise that makes you need to go to the crate often if you listen to the water too much. You win some you lose some.

Eyes closing and a comfortable sleep is here.

Chapter Thirteen

I woke up in the middle of the night missing my life. I am lying in this place I now call my home. This is where I live and I am lonely and sad. Lying with my sweatshirt snuggled up I think about all of the times I had walked out in the woods. I often wonder if Stem had seen me before or I had walked by him while he hid behind a tree.

I feel a cold coming on. Sneezing and clearing my throat I decided to get up and find what I need to make my coffee. I decided to use a clean shirt for the filter and a camping pot I found in the stack of items in the other room. I headed out to the fire and put the water on to warm it up. Getting it to boil may be difficult unless I can get the flame going more.

I have found a tin cup, an extra pan and used a hair tie to bundle up the coffee in the fabric. This was very satisfying and a clearing for my mind. As I poured the hot water over the bundle over and over the coffee started to brew and the smell was amazing. I had nothing to add except a sugar packet that I had found in the duffel. There was a baggie of them and I intended on making them last as long as I could.

I took my new brew back to my cot and sipped at it for a few minutes. My watch was showing 4am and I decided to stay on my cot for a few minutes. I was dreaming on and off of finding a way to leave. Or finding a way to just accept my new life.

And just as I had fallen asleep again for the third time I heard a noise. I heard voices and just stayed in place. I look up and see Stem in the doorway. He seems to be looking at me to see if I am awake.

I say to him quietly, "I am awake, how was your trip?"

He grins with a sneaky looking smile and walks away. That is odd. Maybe he wants me to follow him to see how it went. I sit up too quickly and feel the dizziness come over me. I was sweating and not well. Maybe the coffee was too much. After steadying myself for a moment I went to the crate to get my bearings. I felt sick. After losing my coffee in an upheaval I felt better. It must not be meant to be consumed without a hotter brew.

I found Stem out in the large living area. He was walking towards the water areas maybe so he could clean up. He has a lot of mud and leaves stuck in his hair near his feet. Most of his body hair is very short and seems longer on his lower legs.

I followed him to the water and my voice echoed across the large room.

"How was your trip, are you ok?"

He said, "My trip was good. I brought a gift for you. I wanted to find something to bring happiness to you."

He must think I am crazy. He steps into the water and runs his fingers through his hair. I smile and hand him my soap that I left on the rocks. His smile and his voice are rugged and sweet.

"I will take you to your gift when I finish here." he says. Despite my anxiety and fear of what it could be I smiled back and sat down to wait. My stomach was still a tad bit upset and I was guessing because it was close to time for my monthly. I wonder how he knows me so well so soon. He figured out quickly that I love surprises. Maybe it was because of my last reaction.

I watch him wash and swim. I do care for him and am happy that he has returned safely. With his family away our time will be like the first days I spent with him. Just us. Alone. I liked that idea. He looked at me while he was splashing around and could not take his eyes off of me. He swims to the end and motions me to stand. I walk towards him with the fear of getting his wet hair on me and as usual I go with it.

He pulls me into the water and turns me to face the stone slab. I knew what was coming. I felt my clothing pulled off. He lays me down on my stomach will my legs dangling off into the water and my body heats up. I feel myself enjoying this part of his courting.

This is not something I would have ever expected and I certainly never had this reaction for a very long time with Dave.

I waited and grabbed the stone anticipating the gentle force for the first moment. His hands grabbed my hips and pulled me back. My arm hair now standing on end and my breathing is now heavy. I waited for the moment he would finish. It was always to the point. He had a clear mission and Barka was right there was no real romance as breeding is what breeding is meant to be.

His howl echoed the room and I turned over to look at him.

I grabbed a towel and went over by my seat to hang up my clothes. The blanket was still hanging and was dry. I decided to grab it and head back to my room to get some dry clothes. My nice warm clothes for the day were now wet and I would have to wait until bedtime to wear them again.

As Stem entered fluffing his head with his towel I finished dressing and lacing up my shoes. I stopped by the crate on the way to the doorway and used the baby wipes I had found in my bag. The feeling was nice and soothing.

I followed his lead and walked with his large hand in mine. We went past the guards and he asked me to sit down. He left.

He went around the corner and came back with three more bags! There was a backpack and 2 more duffels. I was so happy. He left again and I sat with the bags in front of me. I pulled the green backpack closer and unzipped the front pocket. I almost cried. I was looking at a cell phone and headphones. This bag was packed and I found a phone. I could use this to make a call. I could get away. If I was to make that choice.

About ten minutes later as I was digging through the bag looking at the new socks and snacks I heard something unusual. It was whining. It was loud whining. And I looked up to see my dog run around the corner with his tie out chain still attached. Stem walked proudly behind and I was knocked over by my sweet girls love. She was so happy to see me. I was so emotional that I just about broke down.

I was happy. I also realized immediately that this meant that Stem was able to get to my home in the fourteen hours he was gone. He knew where I lived. He found his way and found my dog.

Those bags were suddenly unimportant. I had my special surprise and was very happy to hug her again and love her. I went through the doorway past the guards and let her run through the large area. Stem follows behind with my bags. I had to thank him. I turned to him and gave him a large hug and thank you. I took his necklace into my hand and looked at it for a moment. He felt satisfied and content.

As he was before, exhausted. He had to go and rest after his long trip. I felt those old questions coming back. I wanted to ask him about my home and my dog. I decided to leave it alone for now and just enjoy what I could. I took the big floor blanket out and brought it to the big area and as my dog laid down to snuggle I started to make a big plan to go through these bags.

I take out the cellphone and power it on. I wrapped my sweatshirt around it to try to keep the noise down. It was a nice phone and whoever owned it must be missing it by now. The background photo is of a bearded man standing on a mountain. I turned the sound off and muted the settings so I could click on the photos. I could see that there was no service and was not sure if I could dial out or not.

Before clicking on the photos I pressed the phone icon and pressed emergency for 911. It rang one time and then went to a busy signal. The battery was full so I decided to try again. Once again it rang and went to the busy signal.

I clicked on the photo icon and there were thousands. Many photos of fishing trips and hunting. Children and Woods.

It was nice to look at. I opened the camera and was able to see myself. I was not prepared to see that. I looked worn out and dirty. I took a photo of myself.

I tried to open other apps with no success. The phone said no internet connection. I tried the settings. I checked for data. I had no service. I tried 911 once again. Maybe they would get an idea of the location of the phone and come looking for it.

I was not looking forward to the day that someone may come. If they were looking for me and it involved Stem getting hurt that would upset me very much. I wanted to leave and at the same time I felt that my presence here was needed. I know that sounds crazy and I may be mentally unstable and not thinking clearly. In fact I am sure of it. I am unsure and concerned about my entire life.

I spent hours looking through the phone and the bag contents. In just the backpack I had discovered so many useful items that I wanted to keep them all to myself. I put the headphones on and played the music playlist. It was wonderful to hear. There was a little bit of everything and I just let it play on shuffle.

In the backpack I found more snacks, a journal, condoms, keys and a pocket knife. There were also extra headphones, batteries, and a metal coffee cup with lid, umbrella, pens, and plastic shopping bags.

I felt like I was working in a lost and found department. I studied every item. In the bottom was a baggie of chewing gum, tissues, whistle, silverware and eye drops. I also found more toothpaste and toothbrushes. It seems that my dentist will be happy about that someday if I ever see him again.

I placed the most important items back in the bottom to hide and turned the phone off. I sat there thinking about opening the other bags but decided against it for a few minutes and chewed a piece of gum instead. I sure wished I would stumble across some dog food.

I have an abundance of meat so that is not a problem. Where would I walk her to use the bathroom?

I could easily pick it up but that is going to be a big odor problem. The crates do not flush. They are just set above deeply dug holes. I almost wish he would have not found her. She was better off safe at home. Maybe home is not safe. Where were my children or Dave when he went there? Did they leave her tied out when they went to bed?

I do not understand. I feel sick again. I run to the crate with dog underfoot and vomit again. I just do not feel well. I think that I may need to rest and if it continues hopefully we are not too far from Barka or another medical room.

I climb onto my cot and pat my leg to let my sweet girl know it is ok to lay with me. I will just lay my head down for a few minutes and then I will try to find her a water bowl of some sort.

This day was just too much excitement. I have too much nervousness and anxiety. I hid the phone in my pocket to try the call again later. I decided to keep trying.

There may be a way to leave safely without hurting Stem or disclosing their way of living. I will just rest. For a moment. Or two.

Chapter Fourteen

The days went by with no new events. I continued to hoard the items from my new bags that Stem had brought to me. My dog slowly adjusted to the surroundings and I spent a lot of time with her while alone during more of Stems hunting trips. The bulk of the items in the bags were the same items I had already seen from the first surprises he had found for me.

Apart from trying the phone. I spent hours trying to walk around to discrete areas looking for a bar to appear at the top revealing that there was enough service to make a call. I had not considered that the owner may have reported it lost and that it had no service. I kept trying anyway thinking it would someday save me.

The guards were always in place. They never spoke unless spoken to first. I longed for a friend or someone to talk to about my feelings. I was skirted by silence and it was not good for my mental health.

Above ground the authorities were still raking the area for any signs of me. My family had found a way to function with my absence. I was missed but no longer to the point where they could not live their daily lives. As the weeks passed by I was yearning for the searchers to locate me. I am sure that there was dysphoria the day that my dog was missing. They knew she was my great love and it must have made them feel sad and guilty for leaving her unattended long enough to be taken.

Stem returned with new pillages of meat and I suggested that I make a trip to see Barka. I had not been feeling well and had a deep suspicion that my fears have come true. I had witnessed other human women here and also identify that many of the Bigfoot's that I had met in passing may be half breeds as well. It was apparent to me that the families here were all private and yet somehow intertwined in their ideas about evolving.

There were many generations and areas filled with happy families. I did not agree with the process they used to complete their families. Making human work slaves and breeders was a very bold move on their part and also very dominant.

I wondered what happened to those that did not comply with them. Surely they would never be released. Perhaps due to the opportunity they would have to alert those above that they exist. I had never in my years got wind of a captive Bigfoot. I had always believed they were animal in nature. I am sure now that they are not. They have more human traits including intelligence than I could have ever imagined.

Stem said, "I will take you."

I was happy about that offer. I was very worried about seeing the bad ones that had taken me before. I thought about Broken and Hairy Mary. They must be wanderers that live in the common areas. I was not sure how we would leave this area to find our way to Barka.

"Today? You will take me now?" I said.

He took my hand and led me past the guards. I was calm and excited at the same time. I was nervous and anxious. Scared. I calmed myself down to enjoy the walk. Swinging my arm to let him know that I was happy he made the decision to take me. We walked back through the maze of pathways until we reached the original area his family had stayed in. It was filled with new Bigfoot members I had never seen. They must be transitioning also. Just like Stem when he was searching for a mate.

We walked down the pathway past our old room. I could not help but glance in for a moment. There was a young woman lying on the cot. The fire was burning and she was alone. She must be new. She was starting her new life here also. She did not speak as we passed by she only looked with the tears in her eyes that I knew so well.

I wanted to tell her what I knew. I wanted to help her or ask where she was from. I wondered how many others there were being brought in every day. I know there must be hundreds of Bigfoot here. I am disappointed in myself for not knowing more.

As we came to Barkas office Stem helped me to the doorway and then said to her that he would stay close.

I sat on the cot and was relieved after such a long walk to just rest. It took us more than an hour to travel this far.

"I expected to see you soon." she said.

I was so happy to see her. Even though my questions are never answered as quickly as I would like she is always honest with me. She always stays kind and focused on what she does every day here for everyone. I told her that I had not felt well. I told her about my new living quarters and that I was safe. I wanted her to know that I had adjusted well.

"You must know by now that your Breeding with Stem has been a success." she smiled.

I understood what she was saying. I had on several occasions now been the partner in crime for the quick acts of ledge breeding. I was thankful for the short amount of time involved for the act itself. I did not want to go into any details with her but at times it was uncomfortable. It was also exciting. I was torn in between the two on and off.

"I would say that as the cold weather moves in, you can expect to carry your child until the warm weather returns." she continued, "I am sure Stem will be proud and he will see that you are taken care of very well."

I did not doubt that. I knew Stem would be happy and feel proud of his new child when it arrives. I on the other hand was not so sure I was happy to give birth in the conditions here. There would be no lab tests or ultrasounds. There would be no pain medications. I would progress and bear this child on my own with only nature around me.

She was careful to check my skin and my abdomen. She looked at my breasts and my legs. I was not sure what she was looking for but I passed and she gave me another moss tablet to eat. I would not mind more of those as long as there were no wild mushrooms involved.

"Stem you may come in. Em will bear your child when the cold weather ends. Please bring her to me if there are any concerns and I will come to visit when it is time for her to deliver." she said.

He grinned, picked me up and carried me away. He was beaming. We went down the pathway this way and I was hoping that he would set me down at some point to work out my legs a bit more, that were not as muscular as they were when I had arrived.

I have really let myself go. And with that being said, I realize I am nothing more than a frumpy Bigfoot Breeder that lives in a rock and dirt cave. Yes that is my reality.

When I first met him he was kind and timid. He has never strayed from this. He has remained kind and now comfortable with me. He will no longer have the need to breed with me and that will be unusual as I had grown to expect it at the most random times.

I was now one of them. I had fulfilled his goal of becoming the man he was intended to be. As we got closer to our area he set me down. I squinted as he stepped on my toe and laughed at his immediate concern. The weight of his feet felt like a bowling ball and I had become immune to the pain of the unintentional strength he gave out.

Moving along quickly I was happy to see the guards and my dog inside the doorway. He led me in and then stepped back out to speak with them. Bragging rights for future fatherhood was surely something he waited for. He was happy and it made me happy to know that I was the reason for it.

I immediately started planning and thinking about raising our baby. Where would he or she sleep? I am sure that I would have to breastfeed and that worried me due to the fact that I had not had good luck with that in the past. What else could a baby eat to grow besides my milk? I could make some smaller blankets for the baby with the unused men's clothing I had found in my lost and found bags. I do believe there was even an emergency sewing kit in one of them. I may use that to make a small blanket with some squares. I have tiny scissors and thread. A few needles and a dream.

I wondered what would become of me if I was to escape in the condition that I was in. Would my baby be taken away in the name of science? Would I become an outcast or a celebrity? I could just imagine the news stories and invites to talk shows. Life would certainly be different for me up above again. It was like I was torn between two lives. I was not sure I would ever be able to go back again after this. Maybe I was better off here.

I went to my organized stack of bags and found the journal and pens that I had tucked away. I decided to draw some square calendars in the book and to estimate my time spent here and how long it would be before my baby arrived. I had not been told how they calculate days. I had asked and had never received a direct answer.

I know that I spent all of September here. I am sure of that. I tried to count back the days by the activities that I could remember. If I had to guess I would say it could be late October. I decided to start the calendar with November. That would put me at approximately May for delivery. I was not in my right mind with this at all. I felt my heartbeat faster and stopped to breathe for a moment. That would be 7 months for me until I was able to get to this part of my stay here past me.

I did not feel at all like most mothers do. I touched my belly. I felt the size and how it had not really increased at all. I did feel bloated. That is typical I guess. It had been many years since I had a newborn. It was hard to remember all of the signs and the progress made in weeks. I created enough pages of months to go through July and stopped. I was not sure why I would even go that far. I could be free by then.

Stem entered the room and sat down to get the fire started. We had been so busy that it had gone out. I kept busy with my pen and drew some flowers and hearts on my page. He coughed a little and asked if I would like to eat.

I said, "I would like that, yes. I would also like to rest for a while afterwards."

With that sideways grin he grabbed a sack and some warming sticks and asked me to come sit with him and eat. He was very nervous.

I could tell by the way he fumbled with the stick. While he warmed the meat I asked him to wait there and ran for my chocolate stash in my backpack. I was hoping that there was nothing forbidden in my bags that would upset him. He seemed so full of trust to go out and collect them for me without looking inside. He had no concerns about my caring for him. I think he felt confident and self-assured that he was a good provider and would always treat me right.

I ran across the room with my new energy from the excitement and asked him to close his eyes. Of course he did not listen. He looked at me and grunted. I took my hand and gently passed over his eyes to show him what I wanted him to do and he left them closed. I took a piece of my candy bar and broke it off into smaller pieces and asked him to open his mouth. I touched his lips with my hand and pushed the piece in and pinched his mouth shut.

"Now just taste it. Let it melt in your mouth." I said.

He sat there for a few minutes without moving and while it melted I started eating mine. I laughed at him a few times because he had still not opened his eyes.

There goes that trust again. He never doubts me for one moment. I really like that a lot. It is really enjoyable.

"Open your eyes and let's eat." I said while laughing a little more loudly. It was funny and for a moment I think he understood why I was laughing.

Because he smiled.

Chapter Fifteen

More days and weeks had passed by. His family had still not returned and my journal calendar now says January. We had spent the majority of the new winter months swimming and sleeping. It seemed that the colder it got the more he slept. I was ok with that. I liked the time alone to write and craft things with my private stuff. I had given up trying to get a signal for the phone. I had tried so many times and spent so many hours looking through it at photos and the files that the battery was very close to shutting down completely.

That made me a little angry and sad at the same time. I was mad at myself all of the time for landing myself in that well. I was sad that I accepted my new life and never really gave a fight.

There had been no Thanksgiving or Christmas tree. New Years was completely nonexistent. It was winter and we were cozy and warm. The fire was always burning and the warm water steam kept the area nice. It will always feel damp to me. I think that is due to the lack of sunshine. I would give anything to just sit in a chair outside in the sun. There could be snow right now.

The hunting trips were scarce now. He had only left once since he found out I was having his baby. We had more than enough food and my stomach was increasing in size quickly. I estimated that I was about 4 months now and with the fifth month approaching I looked much further along. I felt the baby move a lot. I had no complications and was eager to see Barka more frequently. She would come to see us now. I am spared the long walk.

I let my mind wander more and more about how I will be in a few months with a new baby. There is no hospital and no tests. There is no medical care. Unless you count the moss tablets that I get every visit.

I lay down on my blanket by the fire and count the kicking. I raise my shirt to look at it. I see the guard look in. He keeps turning his head to watch me. I feel like the sight of my bare belly is intriguing to him and I pull my shirt down quietly and look at the fire.

I have learned one very important thing since being taken by the crazy Bigfoot and that is to not provoke or antagonize them. If I kept it up I could easily find myself being bred by a guard and possibly witnessing Stem becoming very violent with him. What a vision that is stuck in my head. I would hope at this point that would never happen.

I stood up to walk for a while and took my dog back to the water. She had her favorite spot there and the guards could not see us. It was private there and peaceful. I really enjoyed soaking my feet in the water and lying on the rock slabs with a thick blanket.

Suddenly I hear a large boom. It sounded like an explosion. Small pieces of the roof and walls were dropping everywhere. It was nothing major. But it was enough to signal me that an earthquake could be happening. It is not tornado season. I am not sure what it could be.

I hear Stem jump to his feet in the next room. I had learned that sound a long time ago due to his size there was never a quiet moment when he started to move around.

He says to me that he will be right back. He heads out towards the doorway to speak with the castle guards. I just dried off my feet and slipped my shoes on enough to scuffle to my cot. I would take a rest for a while, while the men out there locate the source of the loud noise.

It was really quiet except for the noise of Stem talking out there. I could not hear his words but heard a lot of going back and forth about something. I laid still and hugged my dog. I was comfortable and content. I felt the baby move again inside of me. I wondered if it would be a boy or girl. I started thinking of names. I could lean towards the natural side like most of the Bigfoot individuals I have met. Maybe something that was similar to Bushy or Vine. Or a name like Leaf or Stick. No those sounded silly and I would spend some time with my journal in the next few days making lists of great names.

I started to hear more noise after I had slept for a few minutes and decided to go take a look. I walked closer to the doorway and seen Stem over near a large pile of dirt. It was huge. I asked what was happening and seen the guards over by the pile also. We did not always have the same guards. They switched out and even though their sizes were different and hair color I could still barely tell which was which. The two with Stem this afternoon were concerned and looking around quickly.

Stem said, "Em stay back while we are working here. There has been a collapse and the tunnel is gone."

No pathway? How would we leave? I was concerned. How would Barka get here to see me this week? How would the guards go home?

"Ok I will go rest for a while." I said.

I really had no other words. I had never really entertained the idea that all of our areas could cave in at any time. Thank goodness it was just a path. What if it would have been my room? I snuggled under my blanket and once again I found myself in the soundest of sleep when I heard noise again. This time it was not a boom. It sounded like tools. I think they were shoveling. Maybe they were trying to dig through to the path.

I hoped that it was not as bad as it seemed. I felt my baby. I hugged my dog and wished for a new day. I had seen a long night ahead going through my bags looking for more ideas to entertain myself.

It turned out to be a very long night of noise and work for them while I sat by the fire. I marked the day off on my homemade calendar and drew some trees and a little house. I escaped into the drawing I created for just a moment. It felt like a vacation.

For a moment I was away from this place and even though I was safe I had a new worry. I had the worry of being trapped more profoundly than I had felt before.

I listened to the digging and the frustration they had out in the large domed area. It was hard to stay put and not lend a hand. I liked being involved and just letting Stem carry all of the stress from it was hard. I hoped they had encountered this before and would be able to work through it quickly. Maybe residents on the other side were digging as well.

Suddenly I heard another big boom. It did not sound like it came from above but from the dirt filled pathway that had already caved in. I heard yelling and one of the guards yelled for help. I ran faster than I ever thought I could across the great room and seen a larger pile and only Stems hand. He was completely covered by hundreds of pounds of dirt and there was no sign of movement. I fell to my knees and starting digging with my bare hands. I dug and threw dirt as fast as I could. The guard kept digging and the other was also missing.

I tried to uncover the area near his head first. I knew he would not have any air to breathe. He was still not moving. I was able to dig deep enough to uncover his arm and I felt his warmth. I was then making my way up towards his shoulders and head after several minutes. There was so much dirt in his hair. We spent a few more minutes to get his face uncovered and I touched his cheek.

"Stem I am here with you, we will get you out." I said gently.

He did not open his eyes and the guard and I dug for another hour until he was uncovered enough to pull from the dirt. I could not lift him. Even the weight of his arm was too much. He rolled him over and went back to dig more to find his friend. I was crying over Stems face. I was terrified that he would not make it. The thought of being trapped with no more food and no more companionship is too much to take for me at this moment.

I begged him to wake up. I continued to pick the dirt off of his face. I brushed him off and ran back inside to get my water and a towel. I could feel him breathing and his chest was rising from him taking in air. I splashed the cold water on him and kept telling him I was there.

I asked the guard his name. I felt it was time to know this. I needed to feel friendship from someone while this terrible tragedy was going on.

"My name is Ash and I will stay with you and help as long as I can. We have a long way to go. This is very bad." he said.

I appreciated his offer and his serious take on the situation. I continued to wash Stems face and hold his hand.

After several hours, Ash was still digging to look for the other guard and I was exhausted. Stem was still unconscious. I asked if there was any way he could help get him through the doorway near the fire. I would be more comfortable there and could care for him more easily. I went in and cleared my things away. My journal and blankets were in my favorite spot.

As Ash brought him in I rolled up a towel to put under his head and put a cool wet cloth on his forehead. I made my bed and lit the fire and lay there with him all night.

I woke to the sound of moaning. Stem was moving his head back and forth slowly while lying on his back. I reached over and touched his hand. He turned to face me and opened his eyes.

"There was an explosion of some kind and you were buried in the dirt. I was so worried about you. Ash and I dug you out and he brought you in here so you could rest." I said.

In an exhausted voice, he said "I am not sure what happened. Thank you for staying with me. Where is Ash?"

I explained to him that Ash could no longer dig. He became so tired. He was resting in another room. He then sat up and headed to the crate room. He was limping just a small amount but other than that he was ok. I was relieved. When he came back out he told me that the pathway caved in. It was hard to say why unless he was able to go up above and check the area. If that was stable then he would be able to decide if someone had intentionally done this.

Since we were hidden well in our area I doubted that anyone was on the other side. I know the other guards come this way to work for Stem and they may be trying to dig through. I expressed my concern over being trapped and having enough supplies. I did not mention the baby. I was very concerned about that though. What if I needed help from Barka? I was alone without her.

He patted the top of my head and went to look for Ash. I decided to take the dog back by the water and wash my face. Her bathroom area is back that way and I keep it cleaned up daily to avoid any additional smells around me.

Lately my senses were really getting to me. Things that normally do not bother me were starting to. I was feeling sick to my stomach easily from it all also. After some crate time, dog time and wash time I headed back to the fire. I stopped on the way to grab some snack bars I had been saving. I just did not feel like eating the meat this morning. I made small amounts of coffee with my shirt filter invention many times and today was not a good day for that. I just did not feel well.

I decided to let them do what they were going to do out there and just relax. I ate and went to my cot. It was closer to the crate and I had been eating and drinking more. I was gaining a lot of weight in my abdomen and not so much anywhere else. I felt healthy but starved. I needed junk food. I needed a big cake.

I covered up with my hoodie and blanket and just rested like I used to on a Saturday morning. I just let my cares float away. I trusted that Stem and Ash would solve the problem as soon as they were able to check it out again.

My dog jumped up and lay at my feet. What a comforting morning.

All was well at this moment.

I felt it.

Chapter Sixteen

I walked through the great room and heard no noise. I did not see Stem and his family was still away. I was feeling very tired and had marked my journal to show that I was closely approaching my late stages of pregnancy.

I felt big and miserable. I was alone and sad. Stem had been digging his way out of the tunnel for so long that I was starting to lose hope in ever seeing Barka again. I walked through the doorway only to see light through the top of the dirt.

There were no guards or sign of any activity. I pulled my sweatshirt hat over my head to keep the chill away and walked towards the mound of dirt. It was easy to see that they had climbed through and made it to the other side.

Just then my dog ran past me and sniffed her way up the dirt hill. I called her back to me and she just kept returning. I begged her to come back to me and she went over the mound. The past frustration of dog ownership came over me like a flashback. Days in my old home when I had let her out and she bolted through the yard running. The more I called the faster she ran from me. I was not in the mood for a dog chase. I was not in the mood for much on this day and I was feeling close to losing it mentally. I was at a breaking point. I could feel it.

"Solstice, please come back here." I said.

I used my mean voice and demanded that she get back over the hill. I whistled and held out my hand as if I was offering her a treat. I felt my heart drop as she disappeared over the hill. I then seen the tip of her tail vanish as she dropped out of sight and I felt sick.

I tried to climb the dirt as quickly as I could and kept calling her with all of the voice I could find. Please. Please don't go. I was sliding down and climbing back up in a panic. I got to the top and had to lie down to slide through on my back to fit. I slid down into the other side and she was gone. There was no sign of her that quickly. There was no one including Stem or my dog. Everything that was close to me here had vanished.

I sat down at the end of the pathway and broke down into tears. I cried like I had never cried before. I just could not go on one more day with this feeling. The feeling that nothing was ok. I walked a few more feet just wiping my tears with my hands until my eyes were so foggy that I could not see. I wanted her back and I was scared.

I called to her. I prayed in my mind that something would make this ok. I wanted to feel the softness of her fur and to look into her big brown eyes. She was just such a big piece of my heart that I just could not let go of the idea that she may never come back.

I remembered the day that I first got her. She was just 7 weeks old. She was chubby for a lab pup and loved a belly rub. Her belly was so round and cute. She could not even roll back over by herself she was so plump. Years went by that were filled with belly rubs. I discovered something very beautiful about my connection with her and that was this. She woke up every day with the best job in the world. She spent all of her days loving me and that was what she lived for.

She watched my every move. She begged to go for a ride. She loved it when I got the leash out to let her know that it was our time to spend together.

I walked and searched in despair. She was so fast. She could have made it very far by now. I had no idea where these pathways led. I was afraid to go too far. I decided to keep going. I would walk until I found her or found Stem. I felt the dirt on the walls as I walked through letting my fingers leave a mark. I was afraid of getting lost. But I was more afraid of never loving that dog again and feeling her at my feet while I slept.

I came across small empty rooms. A much needed crate room and a maze of pathways. I kept going. I was calling out to her over and over.

Still as I walked there was no sign of life. Not one sign. I felt like I was in an abandoned mine. Where did everyone go? Forgetting everyone else, where did my sweet girl go? Was there an end to these trails of dirt? I walked and walked until I ended up in a large common area that had a worker in it. He looked younger and was stacking rocks. I must have frightened him a little with my appearance and he coward back a little. He did not know what to do or say.

"Do you know Stem? Have you seen a dog run this way? Is there anyone here that I can talk to?" I said frantically.

Please say something. Say anything. I will not hurt you just talk!

He looked at me and said, "Stem was here very early today and went that way. I have not seen a dog or anyone else."

I let the tears roll down my cheeks. I had walked all of that way and this was the way I had chosen. Stem had been here but my dog had not. I thanked him with my shaky voice and went back to find another pathway that Solstice could have taken. I walked for hours and turned around at another dead end. My hope left me. I knew that it was too late. She was gone. My heart was empty. I continued on crying until I reached the dirt hill again. I did not know what to do. If I went over and back in I was giving up and letting her go.

So again I sat at the bottom of the dirt. I ran my fingers through my hair. I looked at my dirty broken nails and nervously went through each one to get the dirt out. I looked at myself in a different way. I felt different and I knew that it was time to make a stand. I could no longer feel this way. I had been kind and submissive to all that were here for my own reasons. It was mostly due to wanting to survive.

I could not do that any longer. I had to become a fighter. I had to find a way home. I had to get out and breathe again. I had to stop crying and be strong. I climbed that hill and headed for my room.

I grabbed that old backpack and filled it with my journal and snacks. I gathered some meat and water. I took dry socks and other items I treasured from those bags.

I held the cellphone that I had given up on and tucked it into my pocket. I threw the backpack on and headed out. I was heading out to take back my life and to also continue searching for my dog.

I felt huge and tired. I walked and walked until I found a place to rest. I hid in a crate room just to close my eyes for a few minutes. I hid because I was not sure if someone would come along that would hurt me. That crazy Bigfoot was still out there. I had not seen Broken or any others since Stem took me to his family's area.

I knew that there was a way out. There was a way

other than the wells because Stem was able to go above. There is an opening or a way. I was determined to find it.

While I lay resting I had no idea that above ground my dog ran through the woods. She had found her way out and as I spent my time searching for her she was running for freedom. I did not know how far we were from my home and she was making progress to town again. I had only hoped if she had escaped that she could find a way back to my neighborhood and that the kids or Dave were there to see her and call her in.

I had a braided fabric collar on her that I had made from old clothing in those bags. I had hoped if she returned they would see this and try to discover where it could have come from.

I continued to stay in the crate room and cry. I cried so much that I knew I was on the brink of just losing my mind. I knew all of the tears would not bring back my family or my dog. I knew too well the feeling of loss. It is so hard sometimes to accept it. I feel for others that have great loss. I know that each day must be so very hard to even get up and move forward for them.

I felt that I was stronger than this. I was not the person that was sitting here in the dirt crying. I was a woman that always knew what she wanted and I was the woman that could fix anything. I lived to solve problems and make a better life for myself.

But here I sit. Broken. Defeated. No one knows how I feel inside. I have no one to talk to. My story cannot end here and yet I have no idea what to do.

I wanted to keep going and searching for a way out. I wanted to find my dog. I needed to know where Stem had gone. I propped my backpack under my head and tucked my arms and hands inside my sweatshirt. I would just lay still and take a short break while deciding what I should do next.

I listened while I rested and there was nothing but silence. No loud footsteps were around me. There were no sounds of voices. I listened for a rumble or noise from above. Today was proof that this underground city was endless and linked together by pathways that were not used by the others regularly.

I knew that it must have led somewhere. I could walk for hours only to discover more uninhabited areas. I also could land myself in a group of unfriendly neighbors.

I sat up and pulled my arms out of my shirt. Tossed my backpack on and used the crate. I sipped some water and stood in the doorway looking at the dirt walls. If I went right I may lead myself to a place where I could not return easily. If I went left I would eventually end up back at Stem's.

I walked to the right and took a bold leap into the unknown. I knew better than to try my own judgement. It was questionable. I walked for almost 2 hours and seen the most beautiful sight that I had seen in months. It was sunlight. There was sunlight beaming out from a hatch door on a dirt wall. The hatch was open just enough to fully light the path well and it had been hard to see most of the way. I walked towards it light it was a victory. It was more than I could have ever hoped for.

As I Looked through the crack I saw rocks. I pulled the hatch door open and had a glimpse of recollection of the first well I fell into and also the second well I had hid in. I was almost too big to fit through the hatch with my belly so large. I managed to get through enough to scoot across the bottom and stood up. I was looking up at the sky. The clouds were so beautiful. It was getting close to late afternoon and the sun was starting to set behind the tops of the trees.

I tried to think of a way out. This well was obviously not in a busy area or it would have someone in it. That seemed a bit out of the ordinary for this place. Everything was monitored and routine. Why would they leave a well unattended that someone could fall into and slip out of the hatch? I looked around at all of the leaves and sticks and thought I may be able to make some type of ladder to climb up if I could get enough limbs. I could use some strips of my shirt to tie around the corners to secure them. I am not sure if this would really work but anything was worth a try. I gathered as many as I could and made a pile.

I squatted down to get back through the hatch and found a corner to lie in. I would spend some time manufacturing something that would get me to the top. I also wanted to explore the area I was in to look for any items that could also help with my plan.

I went back and forth getting sticks and tying them together with the fabric I was ripping off in strips. I wound it around trying to make it as solid as I could. As the makeshift ladder became longer I pulled it through the hatch door. I knew that it would be too long to fit if I waited until it was finished. I squeezed back through the hole and worked on it some more while sitting in the bottom of the well.

I suddenly had felt very happy and energetic. I sang a bit. I enjoyed the fresh air. I felt that this could be my greatest craft project ever. I would be lying if I did not say that I was terrified of what was going on around me. I was scared but driven. I had mixed feelings about the sadness Stem would feel if I was to leave. I was also afraid of leaving and attempting to go home while I was expecting this baby.

There were so many things in my head that I could not think about it any longer. I put it all aside and focused on my project. My body hurt. I was tired and lost. I continued braiding the fabric around the wood. I had to make a decision to use my own shirt to have enough to finish this. I could go without. I had a sweatshirt on over my shirt so I would not have been completely cold and bare.

I was very sure that I had enough fabric with my shirt that I would be able to reach this ladder up to the top. I left the ladder and wandered out into the common area. I looked around for any items that would help me secure the ladder to the wall. I could place a few rocks at the bottom so it does not slide. That seemed easy enough. I collected the rocks I had seen around the area and also stopped back in the corner to sip some water and have a snack.

My baby was moving and that sent me to the crate room I had seen around the corner. I really did not need to go there. There was no one around I could easily just urinate anywhere I wanted. I had said it before when I had walked through the woods and will say it again. This is my day. This is my journey. I am going to enjoy my adventure and do what I want to do. If only I could believe myself when I say it. I have let my confidence sink to an all-time low in my life.

I tied the last knot on my rustic ladder and pushed it up the wall. I leaned it across to the back side so that it could not fall or slide. By doing it this way it may be too short. I would need to get it straight up and down. I looked up into the trees and listened to the birds and the wildlife. I was on my way to walking through the area above. I was so close.

I grabbed my backpack and items to avoid leaving evidence that I had been there and crawled back through the hatch. I pulled the hatch door closed to be sure that I would not be seen if anyone was to go down a path in my direction.

I looked up at my hand tied ladder. I grabbed the branches and stepped on the first step. I wiggled a bit to be sure it felt stable. I placed my foot on the second step and then the third. With each step I wiggled and tested the strength. I had 4 steps left to reach the top of the well. Slowly I took each one until I could get my hands on the top of the stone to pull myself out. I made it! The ladder stayed in one piece and I was sitting at the top of the well. It was a beautiful evening. I stood up to look around and was in an area where there was no sign of others.

There were no buildings. There were no smells of pollution or burning. I was in the center of the woods with nothing surrounding me but trees. There were so many that I was sure this must have been a conservation area or state park. I could have easily been on a farm though. I saw some rock ledges and limestone walls. This was very common for Missouri. I had previously walked through many woods while on trips that had very similar bluffs. They always captured my attention due to my interest in caves and the mystery they hold. I had found my own real life mystery.

My cave searching days were now officially over. Someday I had hoped that this would all be behind me. I would be happy to live to tell my story and cherish it all as my greatest adventure in life.

I walked around in circles afraid of leaving the well. I did not want to get lost and end up in the hills without food or water. It was a very hard decision to make. At that very moment my mind was made up quickly when I hear the leaves moving. I heard sticks breaking. I heard something around me. There was no sight of what it was but it was there. I am afraid to look as the sun is almost gone. It would be nightfall and I was sure it was a bear. I could be a deer but the noise sounded more like a big heavy animal. It did not sound like a graceful doe or a big beautiful buck coming out for a late evening meal. I walked back to the edge of the well and moved the ladder to be sure it was still stable and decided to go back down.

With each step down I felt my hope slip away. I had found a way out and had nowhere to go. I could just leave and take my chances. I would be risking my life greatly by doing this. I stepped down slowly until I had about 5 steps left. After having just a few more I suddenly heard a crack. I heard something break and I fell to the bottom of the well.

I landed on my right shoulder and felt roughed up a little but uninjured. I saw blood on the sleeve of my hoodie. I looked under me and there was none. I looked on my pants and there were no signs of blood there either. I felt my face and my hair. I found the source quickly.

My ear tag had been ripped from my ear. I was still dripping steadily. I looked around for the tag and did not see it. I had no extra cloth or fabric in my bag to press to my ear. I used my sleeve and squeezed my way back out to the large room. It was almost dark out so trying to see at night in these tunnels is much harder than it is with peeks of light here and there. I had been lucky to have found those small lights in the bags Stem had brought to me. I pulled one out of my bag and shined it down the pathway.

I decided to head back to Stems and wait there until he was to return. It would take me a few hours to find my way and fortunately I am the type of person that is pretty good with directions. I must have some type of internal compass that leads me in the direction I need. I would consider that a wonderful gift.

I walked and searched for my way back to Stem. I continued on until I was back completely. I had made it to the large dirt pile and it was different. The pile looked smaller. They must have been working on digging it out while I was away. I did not have to lie down or crawl through it. I was able to step up and over to climb across. I saw right away the guards! I ran towards them while still holding my sleeve to my bleeding ear. I said hello and ran past. Stem was standing past the fire area. He looked upset. I ran through the doorway and went straight to him. I put my head on his chest and cried. I had to cry. It was the only way I could soothe myself after what I had been through for so long here.

I was happy to see him because I felt safe again. I asked him where he had been. I told him my dog had run away over the dirt pile and that I was searching for her. I continued to ask where he was and what had happened to cause the dirt to explode. I was back to my usual rambling. He could sense that I had been scared and worried. He rubbed my head and looked down at my ear. He looked worried and just then he picked me up and carried me to the water area. He sat me down on the rock ledge and used the water to clean my ear. I did not give him any real details about what happened. I kept the secret of my ladder and adventure to myself. He was concerned that my dog had run off. He offered help to find her. I was grateful.

We ended the night by the fire. I had thoughts about my sweet girl and my family. I looked at Stem while we sat there and touched my growing stomach.

I was soon to have a child. I was soon to have his child.

Chapter Seventeen

The final days had arrived. I was not well. I felt sick and sad. I had spent the past few weeks relaxing and enjoying time spent with Stem. I had made a baby bed and during a few more hunting trips he had managed to bring me back a few more bags which helped me have additional fabric and items to create some baby diapers and covers.

It is such a mess for me to try to figure out all of this without going to a real store or doctor. I had a few visits from Barka over the past few days to check my progress. I was so large that I was not sure that I could deliver. I was beginning to think that she may be concerned about the same thing.

I started walking around the rooms more to try to start labor. I went for multiple swims and was cleaning up the best that I could. How does one really clean dirt floors and walls? I kept blankets on my floor areas and washed them to keep them nice and clean. I was fortunate enough to have asked Stem to keep his steps outside of the area. He could really stir up some dust as he moved around.

Just as I was ready to go for a swim Barka came in with her big smile. I asked if she would like to talk back by the water and she agreed. She followed me back and we sat on the rock to talk for a few moments. It was nice to lie on the towels and watch the steam float overhead. I really enjoyed talking to her. She asked me to get into the water so that she may demonstrate how to check myself to see if the baby was close. I had some cramping lately but nothing really major. It had been a while since I had been to a real doctor. It was easy to remember how they checked to see if the baby was close. I just never really understood how they did it.

So I ventured out as usual to try to discover what could be a sign. I felt around. Nothing. I was clueless. I moved slowly out of the water back to my towel and Barka asked if she may check. This may have been the most awkward moment in my entire life. I laid back and let her feel my stomach and other areas. I was looking forward to having my body back and the next step of my journey here.

And there it was. Whatever she had just done caused a big rush of fluid. It was not a small amount. I knew now it was time for something to happen. Perhaps this would be the start of an incredible day. I really did not know what to do next. I knew that incident indicated that my water had broken. It was such a heartbreaking moment for me. I was actually very frightened.

My excitement was greater than the fear and I was immediately ready to go through this experience to get to the next step of my life path. I cried some and Barka said that she would stay with me. She also preferred that we stay near the water.

I sat alone while she went out to talk with Stem. I knew that he would be so thrilled. I wonder if he would be the pacing father type. I was still not sure if he had ever been through this type of situation before. He had never directly said whether he had been in this type of relationship in the past. I assumed that he had not. Considering that he still stayed close to his family and that he does not live away from them. I wondered how he would get word to his family after the baby was here.

He did not come into the area. Barka came in alone and gathered some extra towels over on the ledge. We worked together to make a comfortable spot and she told me when it was time to deliver that I would get into the water. I felt some pressure and cramping.

I felt overpowered by the pain that started to come over me. I lay down with a towel under my head as a pillow. It had been months since I had been able to have real medication. I had found a small amount of headache pills in those old bags but had never dreamed that this type of pain would come to me without some type of relief.

I starting thinking about the day I fell into the well. I remember the other humans I had seen sitting and lying on those cots. I knew what had happened to most of them. They were on the other side of the underground villages. They were workers and breeders. They were

Living lives away from their homes and all of the things that had always brought them happiness. They were not as lucky as I was. I was luckier than I had thought because of Stem. I could have ended up hundreds of miles away with some very bad individuals. I could have been taken with so many other unkind bidders at that first gathering. I was not sure if there were many others that were terribly bad. It seemed as though most were kind and intelligent. They were generous and concerned.

I would have never believed in my lifetime that I would witness what I have. I would have believed a photo on the news but I would have not believed that the underground was the hiding place that so many had searched for over the years. It was never imagined and I fell into it. I fell hard. I lived hard. I missed so much and gained so much.

I screamed in pain. It was too much to take. I could not make it through hours of this alone without love around me. I needed someone to hold my hand and tell me it would be ok. I needed comfort.

All I felt was my body shutter with spasms. It was so hard and I felt like the time would be coming soon to push. Barka checked and said that she felt something. She left the room again while I sat up on the hard towel covered slab.

I slipped into the water myself to try to soothe myself and it was a much better change.

I had seen Stem come in with Barka and knew that it must be time. I felt it.

The huge beautiful little hairy love child was coming and I let out a yell that made Stem step back. I cried and pushed. I yelled and cried some more. I tried to stop and breathe. Right at that moment I felt it. The baby's head was visible. Barka jumped into the water when she seen the blood and she reached down to grab a hold of the baby. She was able to help me breathe and push more until he was here.

The most beautiful little baby was here and I was exhausted and in love. Stem had tears in his large brown eyes and she presented him with his son. According to my internal scale of life he must weigh 11 or 12 pounds.

We shall call him Clump.

Baby Clump.